PUFFIN BOOKS

Morris Gleitzman grew up in England and went to live in Australia when he was sixteen. He worked as a frozen-chicken thawer, sugar-mill rolling-stock unhooker, fashion-industry trainee, department-store Santa, TV producer, newspaper columnist and screenwriter. Then he had a wonderful experience. He wrote a novel for young people. Now he's one of the bestselling children's authors in Australia. He lives in Melbourne, but visits Britain regularly. His many books include *Two Weeks with the Queen*, *Water Wings*, *Bumface*, *Boy Overboard*, *Toad Rage* and *Once*.

# Books by Morris Gleitzman

# Morris Gleitzman

GIVE PEAS A CHANCE

PUFFIN

PUFFIN BOOKS

Published by the Penguin Group
Penguin Books Ltd, 80 Strand, London WC2R 0RL, England
Penguin Group (USA) Inc., 375 Hudson Street, New York, New York 10014, USA
Penguin Group (Canada), 90 Eglinton Avenue East, Suite 700, Toronto, Ontario, Canada M4P 2Y3
(a division of Pearson Penguin Canada Inc.)
Penguin Ireland, 25 St Stephen's Green, Dublin 2, Ireland (a division of Penguin Books Ltd)
Penguin Group (Australia), 250 Camberwell Road, Camberwell, Victoria 3124, Australia
(a division of Pearson Australia Group Pty Ltd)
Penguin Books India Pvt Ltd, 11 Community Centre, Panchsheel Park, New Delhi – 110 017, India
Penguin Group (NZ), 67 Apollo Drive, Rosedale, North Shore 0632, New Zealand
(a division of Pearson New Zealand Ltd)
Penguin Books (South Africa) (Pty) Ltd, 24 Sturdee Avenue, Rosebank, Johannesburg 2196, South Africa

Penguin Books Ltd, Registered Offices: 80 Strand, London WC2R 0RL, England

puffinbooks.com

First published by Penguin Group (Australia), a division of Pearson Australia Group Pty Ltd 2007
Published in Great Britain in Puffin Books 2007

010

Text copyright © Creative Input Pty, 2007
All rights reserved

The moral right of the author has been asserted

Set in Minion
Made and printed in England by Clays Ltd, St Ives plc

British Library Cataloguing in Publication Data
A CIP catalogue record for this book is available from the British Library

ISBN: 978-0-141-32411-1

www.greenpenguin.co.uk

*For Barney and May*

# Contents

# Contents

# Mission Impossible

'**Y**our mission,' said Dad to Jake, 'if you choose to accept it, is to take full command of this operation and to achieve victory using only cunning, daring, ruthlessness and cotton buds.'

Dad didn't use those exact words.

What he actually said was, 'Jake, could you keep an eye on things for a couple of hours? The twins kept me and Mum awake most of the night and we're pooped.'

Jake knew exactly what Dad meant.

He and Mum needed sleep.

A motel could be a noisy place, specially when you owned it and lived in it and never got away from it.

Mum and Dad needed him to keep things quiet. It was a big responsibility for someone who'd recently been voted the biggest daydreamer in year six.

'I accept the mission,' said Jake.

Dad gave Jake a grateful but weary smile and tiptoed into the bedroom.

Jake held his breath, hoping Dad wouldn't trip over yesterday's underpants and wake the babies.

He didn't, and the babies were still asleep a few minutes later as Jake sat in the big leather chair in the office and reviewed the situation.

Everything was quiet.

The guests were all checked out or at the beach. Sharnelle and Patsy who cleaned the units had finished and gone. *Out Of Order* signs in Jake's neatest writing were on the ping-pong table, the laundry, the ice machine, the swimming pool and the crazy golf, all three holes. The rattly door on the cold drinks cabinet in the office was wedged firmly and silently shut with cotton buds.

Jake glanced at the clock.

Two-fifteen.

With a bit of luck, nobody would want to check in for at least two hours. Everything would stay peaceful as long as a sea breeze didn't spring up and make the sheets on the line flap too loudly.

Mission accomplished.

Jake couldn't hear a peep from Mum and Dad's room.

Not even a snore.

He looked proudly through the office window at the big sign out the front.

*Off-Highway Motor Lodge.*

*Quietest Motel In Town.*

Which it is, thought Jake, when I'm running it.

He wondered whether to quietly get the ladder and a red marker pen and underline the *Quietest Motel In Town* bit. Before he could, three cars roared past the reception window and screeched into the parking area.

Jake leaped out of the chair with the lithe grace and superb reflexes of Tom Cruise. Or would have done if he hadn't hooked his foot in a worn patch of carpet and gone sprawling.

Jake picked himself up, glared at the carpet with the silent indignation and bruised elbows of Tom Cruise, spat out a bit of carpet fluff and peered through the window at the cars.

At first he thought they were the very thing he didn't want. A gang of early check-ins. Then he saw he was wrong. They were the other thing he didn't want. Units 7, 8 and 9 back early from the beach.

Several mums and dads and lots of little kids were getting out of the cars. Slamming the doors. Chattering loudly.

Jake's thoughts raced so fast he didn't even have time to compare them to Tom Cruise's.

Perhaps, he said to himself, units 7, 8 and 9 have just forgotten their sunblock. Perhaps if I help them find it they'll go back to the beach.

Jake hurried outside.

A mum in a green beach smock and sun-visor

slammed one of the car boots, turned, saw Jake approaching and glared at him.

Jake hoped he'd got that wrong. He hoped she was actually glaring past him at the sign out the front and realising that this was the quietest motel in town and thinking that her kids shouldn't be dragging their plastic spades along the ground so noisily.

She wasn't.

She was glaring at Jake.

'Oi,' she said, jabbing her finger at him. 'Why didn't you tell us that beach hasn't got a shark net?'

Jake was stunned.

Shark net?

The beach was the shallowest beach on the coast. It was famous for its shallowness. If you walked the length of three footy fields out to sea, the water was still only up to your ankles. A shark would need a lift from the rescue helicopter to get anywhere close to the beach.

Jake started to explain this.

Then he stopped.

The rest of the adults and kids were heading for the swimming pool.

'This sign reckons the gate's out of order,' one of the dads was saying. He pushed the pool gate open. 'Seems OK to me.'

They all crowded into the pool enclosure.

Jake hurried after them.

He knew he had about five seconds to think

4

of something before they all started throwing themselves into the water and yelling and splashing and waking up Mum and Dad and Gwen and Mabel and making Jake's mission completely impossible.

Dirty water.

That's it, thought Jake.

I'll tell them the pool water's dirty and not safe to swim in.

Except there was one little problem. The pool was clear and blue and sparkling. Dad was a genius with pool chemicals. He liked to say you could eat your dinner off his pool if you didn't mind soup.

Jake stood helplessly in the pool enclosure, surrounded by adults and kids stripping down to their swimmers. He wished he had Tom Cruise's Hollywood screenwriters to tell him what to do next.

But he didn't.

And one of the little girls was clambering onto the diving board.

Before Jake could stop her, one of the mums did.

'Charlene,' said the mum. 'Get off that. You'll hurt yourself. Come over here in the shade.'

'But I want to swim,' said the little girl.

Several of the other kids were sitting on the edge of the pool, dangling their legs in the water.

'Come away from there,' said one of the dads. 'That water could be filthy. You can never tell with motel pools. Not without a microscope.'

Jake looked admiringly at the dad.

Brilliant, he thought. You should be a Hollywood screenwriter.

The kids didn't look like they thought it was brilliant. They whinged and moaned and dragged themselves away from the pool. They stood dejectedly around the feet of the adults, who were stretched out on sun loungers under umbrellas.

'Can we do crazy golf then?' said one of the little boys.

Jake looked anxiously at the Hollywood screenwriter dad. He seemed to have fallen asleep. Jake scrambled to think of something. *Out Of Order* signs didn't work with this lot.

To his relief, he saw that one of the other mums was on the case.

'No crazy anything,' she said to the little boy. 'I'm not having you taking your eye out.'

'Ping-pong then,' said one of the little girls.

'Too dangerous,' said another dad. 'I read about a kid who choked on a ping-pong ball.'

Jake stared at him, grateful but also puzzled.

Choked on a ping-pong ball?

You'd have to have a windpipe the size of a spa bath waste duct.

Then Jake realised what was going on.

He'd heard Mum and Dad talking about this. How the modern world was making everyone feel scared, parents included. Mum reckoned it was because of global warming and terrorism and war and crime and pollution. Dad reckoned it was also

6

because of bushfires and drought and those TV ads about germs that live on insects and kids.

Mum and Dad are right, thought Jake. People are even bringing their fears on holiday with them.

Jake thought that was a shame, but at least it made people nice and quiet.

He tried to hurry away before the green-smock mum started yelling at him about something else and woke Mum and Dad and the babies.

He almost made it, but one thing stopped him.

The sight of all the little kids sitting under umbrellas, miserable and bored.

Poor things, thought Jake. Not much of a holiday.

He wondered if there was anything he could do to cheer them up.

Quietly.

'Psst,' he said to the kids, kneeling down. He signalled for them to kneel down next to him.

Rows of tiny sugar ants were streaming out of the cracks in the concrete. The kids crowded around, curious.

'Those aren't bull ants, are they?' called an anxious dad's voice from a sun lounger.

'No,' said Jake, trying to demonstrate that it was possible to have a conversation in a quiet voice. 'They're coastal racing ants. But they're very shy and they only race if the conditions are right. They need lots and lots of absolute silence.'

He let one of the ants clamber onto his finger.

'This is my champion,' he whispered to the little kids. 'Antelope Flyer. He can beat any ant here.'

The little kids' eyes lit up.

They chose an ant each and Jake marked out a race track in the dust.

'They're off,' he whispered. 'Shhh.'

The race started.

Jake was impressed. As the ants scampered, the little kids were busting with excitement, but not one let out a squeak.

Brilliant, thought Jake. I should have thought of this ten minutes ago.

Then suddenly there were lots of squeaks. Jake looked behind him. The squeaks weren't coming from the little kids. They were coming from the mums and dads who were all crowding around as well.

Oh dear, thought Jake with a twinge of panic.

He silently begged the parents to control themselves.

They didn't.

'Go,' yelled one of the dads at his daughter's ant. 'Go, go, go, go, go.'

'That's us in the lead,' yelled a mum. 'Hey, not fair. Your brute of an ant kicked our ant.'

'That's not your ant,' shouted another mum. 'That's our ant. Charlene trod on your ant.'

Jake's panic was more than a twinge now.

'Please,' he hissed at units 7, 8 and 9. 'Argue quietly.'

8

They didn't hear him.

Jake prayed things would quieten down once the race was over.

'Go faster,' he whispered to the ants.

Things didn't quieten down once the race was over.

'Nathan's ant won by a mile,' yelled a dad.

'No way,' yelled another dad. 'That's Nathan's loser ant back there going round in circles.'

Jake felt like throwing himself in the pool and just letting himself sink. And taking the whole noisy bunch with him.

This was all his fault.

'Loser, eh?' Nathan's dad was yelling. 'Well you won't say loser when Nathan thrashes your lot at table tennis.'

Before Jake could stop them, the whole group stampeded over to the games room and crowded around the ping-pong table where four kids slugged the ball at each other and the adults whistled and cheered.

Jake was frantic.

The games room was even closer to Mum and Dad's room than the pool.

'Please,' he begged the group. 'Two babies and two exhausted parents are trying to sleep and they can't use sleeping pills because Mum's allergic and Dad only uses herbal medicine.'

But units 7, 8 and 9 weren't listening.

The game ended and a bitter dispute broke out

about the score-keeping. The parents of the losing team flung out a challenge to the parents of the winning team and suddenly the whole group was surging towards the crazy-golf course.

Jake had a disaster-movie-sized jolt of anxiety.

The first crazy-golf hole was right outside Mum and Dad's window.

Jake hurried after units 7, 8 and 9 as their voices echoed around the entire motel.

He could kick himself.

He should have seen this coming.

Dad was saying only recently that some parents' global fears were making them incredibly competitive about their kids. Wanting their kids to always come first so their kids would be better at surviving in a tough world.

Something like that.

Mum had been a bit doubtful, but Jake could see now that Dad was right.

These mums and dads from units 7, 8 and 9 were fearful, but they were also very competitive.

Olympic competitive.

Footy grand final competitive.

Nicole Kidman and Katie Holmes playing crazy golf in Hollywood competitive.

Jake knew he had about five seconds to think of something before a golf ball smashed through Mum and Dad's bedroom window.

He had an idea.

He flung himself into the middle of units 7, 8

and 9, who were squabbling noisily over who got to use the crazy-golf club first.

'Listen,' he yelled as loudly as he could, but facing away from Mum and Dad's room. It was a trick he'd learned from teachers. Sometimes, to get quiet, you had to make a lot of noise first.

Units 7, 8 and 9 went quiet.

Jake knew he had about two seconds before they went noisy again. This had to be good. Unlike Tom Cruise, he didn't have a special effects team to fake it.

He pointed over to the sign at the front of the motel.

'See where it says *Quietest Motel In Town*?' he said. 'Well, there's another motel over the other side of town who reckon they're quieter than us.'

It was true.

When Dad had put the sign up, the Parkside Slumber Inn had complained to the council.

'That's why,' said Jake, 'we at the Off-Highway Motor Lodge offer a prize each day to the quietest family staying with us.'

Units 7, 8 and 9 thought about this.

'What prize?' said one of the kids.

Jake gulped. He hadn't got quite that far with the idea.

Then he saw that the parents didn't care what the prize was.

'You've lost,' said the green-smock mum to the other parents. 'My kids can be quieter than your kids any day.'

The parents all glared at each other.

Silently.

So did the kids.

Jake held his breath, hardly able to believe it. The whole group were making their way back towards their units on tiptoe, kids with their hands over their mouths, parents pausing only to slip off squeaky shoes.

Jake grinned.

Let's see Tom Cruise have an idea like that, he thought. Even with Nicole Kidman and Katie Holmes to help him.

It was fantastic.

The whole bunch of them, the yellers and the moaners and the arguers, weren't making a peep.

Jake glanced up at the motel sign.

Have to change that now, he thought.

*Quietest Motel In The World.*

Then suddenly the silence was shattered. Not by the parents and kids of units 7, 8 and 9. By a noise far louder than anything they'd come up with.

Two babies howling.

Everyone froze.

Everyone looked at Jake and frowned.

Jake glanced at his watch.

Ten to three.

Oh well, he thought. Forty-three minutes of unbroken sleep is better than nothing. Mum and Dad are always saying that.

Tomorrow he might be able to get them an hour.

For now, though, he had a motel to run.

Units 7, 8 and 9 were muttering to each other.

Jake thought fast.

The important thing was to make sure nobody went into the office and pestered Mum and Dad while they were getting up and feeding the bubs.

Easy.

'Hey,' Jake yelled to units 7, 8 and 9. 'You lot might be good at ant racing and ping-pong and crazy golf, but I'm the fastest swimmer round here.'

Jake took his t-shirt off and sprinted over to the pool. He glanced back, saw he had a crowd of competitors at his heels, smiled to himself, and dived in.

# Paparazzi

I crouch inside the front door, waiting for Kevin. I'm pretty nervous. That's why I'm chewing my nails. Yuk. This new nail polish looks good but it tastes revolting.

I've never done anything like this before. Usually on a Saturday afternoon I'm hanging out at Madonna's place or somewhere. But a friend needs me, that's why I've decided to do this. I just have to be careful I don't ruin everything by being seen.

There are paparazzi everywhere.

That's what Kevin reckons they're called. People who chase after you with cameras, desperate to get your picture, tripping over things, bumping into each other, invading your privacy, yelling at you to pull a funny face or sing something.

Why do families always do that?

Paparazzi sounds like an Italian word. I don't know what the *razzi* bit means, but I bet the *papa* part is because the person at the front with the biggest camera is usually your dad.

My mobile's ringing.

Two rings.

That's Kevin's signal. He must be almost here.

I open the front door and check for grown-ups. I hate to think what Mum and Dad would do if they saw me like this.

When I checked earlier, Dad was in the back yard trying out his new handicam. Mum was taking snaps of him on her digital cause she reckoned he looked so funny trying to video insects and walking into the washing.

From the sound of her giggles he must still have a bra on his head.

I hope they don't wake Daniel. Dan's not really into photos, but he'll always grab a couple with his mobile if there's a chance of getting his little sister into trouble.

The front yard is clear.

I pull the paper bag over my head and half walk half run down the front path.

Oh no, I haven't made the eye holes big enough.

I can't see anything either side of me.

My main worry is Mrs Kyneton next door. Her son got her a six megapixel 3G Nokia for Christmas and she's been putting the whole suburb on her blog ever since.

I don't think she's seen me.

I can't hear anyone yelling 'say cheese'.

What I can hear is Kevin's brother's car wheezing and spluttering as it gets closer.

I hope Kevin's right about it being more mechanically reliable than it sounds. It looks fantastic, a gleaming light-blue 1982 Valiant that always gets photographed at car shows, but looks aren't going to help us today.

The car squeaks to a stop. Kevin's in the front next to his brother. He winds down the window.

'Haul butt,' he says.

Even though I'm sweating with tension, I smile inside my paper bag. Kevin's got hair gel on. He thinks it makes him look like Brad Pitt. It does a bit, but his voice is even squeakier than the car.

'Hurry up,' says Kevin, starting to sound panicked.

I yank the back door open and scramble inside. The car roars away at high speed. That's what I wish it was doing. Actually it chugs away slowly.

'G'day Nat,' says Holly.

Holly is lying across the back seat, her head in a pillowcase. She squeezes over and I lie down next to her so nobody can see us from outside the car.

'Hi Natalie,' says Madonna.

Madonna is lying on the floor behind the front seats. She's got her head wrapped in a towel. It's her sister's sports towel from school. I can see the name tag. Beyonce Crutchley.

'Is it me,' says Madonna, 'or is it hot in here?'

'Sorry,' says Kevin's brother. 'Heater's jammed. I can't turn it off.'

'This isn't hot,' says Kevin. 'I had a go in a spin-dryer once and it was much hotter than this.'

None of us say anything.

Kevin is known all through grade six and most of grade five for exaggerating. It's what you have to do when you're the youngest of eight.

Suddenly the brakes slam on and I roll off the back seat onto Madonna.

'Ow,' she says.

'Sorry,' I say, and try to shift my bony bits.

'Does anyone know anybody with a yellow Corolla?' says Kevin's brother. 'It's blocking our way. There are people inside with cameras and they're waving at us. I think they want us to get out.'

My paper bag deflates. So does my chest.

It's my rellies. They must have come round the corner and seen me as I was getting into the car.

'It's my nan,' I say. 'And my Auntie Pru and Uncle Andrew. They've come over to take pictures of the Christmas clothes they gave me, but they're not meant to be here till this evening.'

'Paparazzi,' says Kevin. 'They don't care whose lives they wreck. I'll handle them.'

He gets out of the car.

'Kevin's amazing,' says his brother. 'He can lie his way out of anything. I've got videos of him doing it.'

Carefully I kneel up, not on Madonna, and peep out the window.

Kevin is yelling at Nan through the windscreen of the Corolla.

'It's an emergency,' he shouts. 'We've got to get to the hospital.'

Me and Holly look at each other through our paper bag and pillowcase eye holes.

Why is he telling them the truth?

In the Corolla, Nan looks puzzled too. She might not have her hearing aid turned up.

Auntie Pru winds down her window and points her camera at Kevin. It's the big one she uses for her wildlife photos on holiday. Kevin sees her and puts his hands up over his face and scurries back into our car.

'Don't worry, Kevin,' says Holly. 'You tried.'

'It's not my fault,' said Kevin indignantly. 'Look at the size of that zoom lens.'

None of us say anything, but we all know how he's feeling. We've all been caught by paparazzi not looking our best. We've all had our pimples and baggy track pants plastered across family slide nights and aunties' websites.

'They're backing up,' says Kevin's brother.

We chug off again.

I flatten myself onto the back seat, hoping they didn't hear what Kevin said about the hospital.

Why didn't he say we were going to the mall or somewhere?

It's not Kevin's fault. He must have panicked. I'd probably have done the same. Dealing with the paparazzi is just so stressful. I don't know how Angelina Jolie and that lot cope.

'Nat, keep your head down.'

Holly is hissing at me because I'm peeping out the car window.

I know she's right, but I can't help it. We're passing what's left of Tara's house and even though I've seen it heaps of times since the fire I can't stop myself looking.

Tara is the only kid in our class whose house has ever burned down.

A great big house turned into a pile of scrap and ash by a bunch of candles.

'Sheesh,' says Kevin's brother, slowing down and staring. 'I wouldn't mind getting a picture of that.'

'Not now,' pleads Kevin. 'We're on a deadline.'

'Yeah, yeah, I haven't forgotten,' says Kevin's brother. 'Keep your gel on.'

We don't stop.

I puff out my paper bag with relief.

But I don't blame Kevin's brother for wanting a picture. Each time I see the remains of Tara's burnt house I'm shocked because it's so much worse than I remember.

For example, I'd forgotten that the tiles in Tara's upstairs bathroom were pink. They're stacked up on the front lawn now, and most of them are singed and scorched and black round the edges.

Which is really sad because it was one of the

nicest bathrooms I've ever been in.

But of course it's not as sad as what's happened to Tara.

'Poop.'

Kevin's brother is swearing.

The car's stalled and he can't get it started again. He pumps the pedal and the engine whines like a kid with pillow hair who doesn't want to be in a family photo.

'Are we out of gas?' says Kevin, who likes to use American words whenever possible.

'Battery's going flat,' says his brother. 'I need a push.'

'I'll handle it,' says Kevin and jumps out.

We don't even wait for him to try. Kevin's built like a TV aerial and even if he could move the car on his own he'd probably rupture one of his very skinny internal organs.

Plus we've got to be at the hospital in less than ten minutes.

'Keep your heads covered up,' Holly says to me and Madonna as we get out of the car.

She doesn't have to remind me. My paper bag is firmly on. To be sprung now would be a disaster.

We all push as hard as we can and the car starts moving.

'Hey,' yells a voice. 'Look. Kev's girlfriends have gone Islamic.'

I recognise the voice.

Rocco Fusilli.

I swivel my head and glare at him through my eyeholes. The one kid from school I hoped would be somewhere else today. Like Antarctica. But there he is, taunting us with his mates. They've got their mobiles out and as we break into a trot, pushing the car, they chase us and take pictures.

'Ignore them,' mutters Holly.

'You're invading our privacy,' Kevin yells at them. 'It's against the law. My dad's a cop and he's watching you on the police satellite.'

Rocco and his mates just laugh.

Kevin is always doing that, exaggerating about the surveillance capacity of the police. Everyone knows that compared to rellies with cameras, most law enforcement agencies can't compete.

The car gives a big jolt and the engine splutters into life.

'Get in,' yells Holly.

We all clamber in and chug away from Rocco and his paparazzi pack.

I flop down in the back with Holly and Madonna. Inside my paper bag I'm sweating.

Just my luck.

I've got the most important photo session of my life coming up and I think my make-up's running.

We bump and totter into the hospital lift. Just the four of us because Kevin's brother has to stay with the car in case it gets scratched.

There are two nurses in the lift.

They stare at us.

I can feel Madonna shuffling nervously behind me and I know why. What if there's a hospital security regulation forbidding visitors to have their heads in bags or pillowcases? What if the nurses ring an alarm bell? What if security guards are waiting for us when the lift doors open and we don't even get to see Tara?

'Hi ladies,' says Kevin to the nurses, who glare at him sternly.

He's got courage, Kevin, for a skinny youngest kid in a big family.

'Don't be alarmed,' he says to the nurses. 'We're here to make a patient feel better.'

The nurses think about this, then both grin at him.

'Fair enough,' says one. 'They say laughter's the best medicine.'

'Which is why,' says the other, 'I predict a complete recovery when the patient sees your hair.'

The lift doors open and we drag Kevin out before he can get defensive about his gel.

As we hurry along the corridor I catch a glimpse of Tara's dad up ahead, going into Tara's ward.

I take a deep breath and keep going.

We knew Tara's rellies would be here for such an important occasion. The surprising thing is that her dad hasn't got his camera round his neck. Out of all our parents, he's the biggest photo fanatic. That's why Tara's house had so many burning candles in it, so their Christmas family pictures would look extra atmospheric.

On second thoughts, after what happened, he's probably gone right off photography.

We stop outside Tara's hospital room and peek cautiously in.

And nearly die.

It's not just Tara's rellies who are crowded around her bed. My mum and dad are there too. And Holly's. And Madonna's.

Kevin's aren't, but with eight kids they never are.

Mum and Dad and the others are staring at us.

None of them have got their cameras.

It's OK, I say to myself. Stay calm. We knew there was a chance this might happen. Everyone must have decided to keep cameras away from Tara.

I glance at Kevin. He pats his pocket.

'It's cool,' he says.

'G'day Nat,' says Mum uncertainly. 'Auntie Pru told us you were coming here and we guessed it must be Tara's special time so we thought we'd come and help cheer her up too. Why have you got a bag on your head?'

I don't say anything, partly because I'm a bit dizzy now the big moment is close and partly because a doctor is bending over Tara's bed, slowly unwinding the bandage from around her face.

We all stop looking at each other and anxiously

watch the doctor and Tara.

It feels like nobody's breathing in the room, except Kevin, who's looking a bit pale and like he might faint.

The last bit of bandage drops away from Tara's chin.

'Good,' says the doctor. 'That is good. It is. It's very good.'

Nobody else says anything.

It's as bad as we thought it would be.

The beautiful smooth skin on Tara's face isn't smooth any more and it hardly even looks like skin. It's bright red and cracked and flaky. And her hair, her long fair hair which was probably the most photographed hair outside Hollywood despite how Tara used to come up with some really clever hiding places to get away from her dad's camera, her hair isn't long any more.

It's short and very patchy.

You can see bits of her scalp.

'Give it a few weeks,' says the doctor to Tara. 'Few weeks and you'll be right as rain. Two months tops.'

Slowly, her hand shaking, Tara picks up the mirror on her bed and looks at herself.

I have a weird thought.

Can people whose faces have been burnt still cry?

They can. Tara's eyes are filling with tears as she looks at her reflection. I glance at Holly and Madonna through my eyeholes.

This is the moment.

I pull my paper bag off my head and Holly removes her pillowcase and Madonna unwraps her towel. We all stand there in front of Tara and let her see us.

I've prepared a speech about how she'll always be our friend no matter what she looks like. But when I see the expression on her face as she stares at us through her tears I know I don't need to say anything.

I glance at Holly and Madonna.

I was right, our make-up has run, but I reckon we still look pretty good. Madonna's mum prefers orange lipstick, so Madonna's face isn't as red as Tara's, but Holly's is. And because we smeared the lipstick onto our faces really thickly and blasted it with our hairdryers, it's cracked and flaky and looks exactly like the real thing, specially on our foreheads.

I'm so glad we decided to give ourselves these short and patchy haircuts and shave our eyebrows off.

We look at Tara.

Tara looks at us.

Yes. It's working.

Tara isn't crying any more. She's even managing a smile.

'Thanks,' she whispers.

Mum and Dad and the other parents are staring at us like the doctor has just given them a really strong anaesthetic that knocks you out with your eyes open.

When it wears off there's a good chance they'll be totally furious. Me and Holly and Madonna know this, but we think it's worth it.

The colour has come back into Kevin's face. Not as much as we've got, but at least he won't need oxygen.

I give him a nudge and he fumbles in his pocket. He pulls out his dad's camera and pushes it into Tara's dad's hands.

Then me and Holly and Madonna and Kevin go over and hug Tara and sit on the bed with our arms round her so the grown-ups, when they recover, can take our photo.

# Greenhouse Gas

Today is a very big day for our family.

Me and Grandpa are both getting honoured. Grandpa's been voted Australian Of The Year and I've been voted Young Australian Of The Year. Plus we're getting a ten-metre-high concrete tomato. Nobody in our family's ever won anything before except scratchies so everybody's very excited.

But there's a problem.

Grandpa has jumped into the sea again and I'm out in the boat trying to find him.

'It's one-thirty, Grandpa,' I yell. 'You're being honoured in an hour and Mum reckons if you're not in your best pants by two-fifteen she's gunna get Andy Wicks to demolish the big tomato with his bulldozer and use the bits of concrete to build a new toilet block in the caravan park.'

I pause, out of breath.

All around me the calm surface of the sea

shimmers in the sunlight like a massively large plasma telly lying on its back. I used that description in my history project, but I only got six out of twenty.

I stare at the water.

I'm looking for bubbles.

Grandpa had fried tomatoes for breakfast as usual. When he goes snorkelling in the ocean after breakfast you can sometimes spot his gas bubbles. You have to make sure they're his bubbles, though. Once I tried to tell a big jellyfish it was morning nap time.

'Grandpa,' I yell again. 'Dad said to remind you that this is the proudest day in the entire history of our town, so try not to blow off at the ceremony.'

I peer at the sea.

'I'll try not to, young Dougie,' says a voice behind me. 'But my botty wind is the least of our worries.'

I turn round.

Grandpa is hanging onto the other side of the boat, treading water and pushing his snorkel mask up from his face.

'I wish you hadn't found me,' he says quietly.

I nod.

I know what he means.

I wish I hadn't found him either, not yet. I wish I could stay out here for another few hours looking for him. I wouldn't even mind chatting with a jellyfish or two. That way me and Grandpa could both miss the ceremony.

Grandpa drags himself into the boat.

Sadly I help him.

We don't have to look at each other to know we're both feeling the same thing.

We don't want to be Australians Of The Year.

I row the boat towards the jetty.

'Careful, Dougie,' says Grandpa as we get into shallow water.

He always says that. It's because of the barbed wire fences just below the surface. This part of the sea used to be all sheep paddocks.

'It's OK, Grandpa,' I say quietly as I steer us past the roof of a submerged shearing shed. 'You can trust me.'

I always say that.

Grandpa usually smiles to himself and says 'yeah, I know', but today he doesn't.

He's frowning and concentrating on picking a bit of seaweed out of his ear. I can tell he's thinking about things.

I know how he feels.

I'm thinking about things too.

'We'll have to own up,' says Grandpa. 'Tell them we don't deserve to be Australians Of The Year.'

My guts go tighter than a sheep fence when a shark swims into it.

But I know Grandpa's right. If we accept these honours we'll spend the rest of our lives feeling guilty.

'If we confess,' I say, 'what'll happen to us?'

'Don't know,' says Grandpa.

Nor do I.

I don't want to think about it. Instead I concentrate on helping Grandpa tie the boat to the jetty.

'We'd better hurry,' I say. 'Mum's having a meltdown.'

I point over towards the house.

Mum's on the verandah, waving to us like an octopus stuck on a windmill. I used that description in my English assignment, but I only got seven out of twenty.

'Three cheers for Noel and Dougie Webber, the tomato heroes of Australia,' says the woman from the government.

There's a big crowd in front of the stage next to the surf club and they all give big cheers. Including my teachers, who still don't understand how a person who's never got more than eight out of twenty can be Young Australian Of The Year.

They don't have to worry.

I can't be.

I wish I could sneak off this stage and creep out of town and never come back. But I wouldn't make it. Hundreds of friends and neighbours are watching, and thousands of city folk from the caravan park.

Anyway, I can't leave Grandpa here to confess on his own.

The cheers die down, almost. Then Mum and Dad realise they're the only people still cheering and stop too. It's not their fault. They're just so proud. When they heard somebody was coming down from Federal Parliament House in Alice Springs to give us our prizes, they nearly cacked themselves.

I wish I didn't have to do this to them, but I do.

Grandpa, who's standing next to me, squeezes my hand.

'You OK?' he whispers.

'I think so,' I say.

The woman from the government is speaking into the microphone again.

'We may have lost the battle against global warming and melting ice-caps and rising sea levels,' she says. 'We may have lost our big cities, but thanks to Noel and Dougie Webber, we haven't lost the battle to feed ourselves.'

The crowd cheers again.

From up here I can see that heaps of people are having picnics and doing their cheering with their mouths full. I can see tomato pizzas and tomato sandwiches and lots of sun-dried-tomato burgers dripping with tomato sauce.

As the cheering dies down, I can also hear the faint sound of thousands of puffs of gas escaping from thousands of bottoms. It's what happens these days when crowds get excited.

And, to be honest, even when they don't.

'Five years ago,' says the government woman,

'a very clever little boy found something very special in his dad's paddock. A native Australian tomato plant that had never been discovered before. The boy's grandfather put its seeds into pots and, thanks to his skill as a gardener, got them to grow. And did they ever grow. They produced ten times more tomatoes per plant than any other type of tomato anywhere. And the rest, as we know, is history.'

I can feel myself blushing, partly because the whole crowd is clapping me and Grandpa, and partly because in a moment I'm going to have to confess to a very big lie.

'Last year,' continues the woman from the government, 'Australia exported nearly a million tonnes of tomatoes to help feed the world.'

More cheering.

More gas escaping from well-fed tummies.

As usual, nobody even notices. That's the thing about botty gas. People start off being polite and pretending it's not happening, and then after years of ignoring it they don't even notice it any more. Not even when it's erupting all around them.

Me and Grandpa notice it.

We notice it a lot.

Mum and Dad do as well, probably because Grandpa goes on about it when he's had a few glasses of tomato wine.

'It gives me great pleasure,' says the woman from the government, 'to unveil this monument to two very special Australians.'

Her assistant puts down his briefcase and grabs hold of the ropes attached to the big tarpaulin. He pulls on them and the tarpaulin slides down and ends up in a heap at his feet.

A bit like my insides.

That's what it feels like.

We all stare up at the Big Tomato. It's the tallest man-made structure in town except for the surf lifesaving tower, and it's definitely the brightest. Ken Bullock in the hardware store was mixing red paint for days.

When the crowd quietens down, as much as any crowd these days can, the woman from the government steps closer to Grandpa.

'And now,' she says, 'please welcome this year's Australian Of The Year, Noel Webber.'

She holds the microphone out to Grandpa, who doesn't even see it.

He's staring over at the shimmering ocean with a smile on his face, which is what he spends most of his time doing when he's not actually swimming or snorkelling. Mum reckons his brain might be a bit waterlogged, but I know that's not it.

Think about it. For the first sixty years of Grandpa's life, this town was hundreds of kilometres inland. Grandpa only ever saw the sea on telly. Now, thanks to melting ice and rising sea levels, we're a coastal resort.

Grandpa can't believe his luck.

None of us can.

We're happier than wallabies in wellies, which is a description I included in my science essay, but I only got four out of twenty.

I give Grandpa a nudge. He sees the microphone and takes it. We look at each other. Neither of us feels very happy right at this moment.

In front of the stage, lots of media cameras are pointed at us.

'Ladies and gentlemen,' says Grandpa. 'Thank you for your kindness, but I can't accept this honour. I don't deserve to be Australian Of The Year.'

People are gasping.

Bits of tomato sandwich are dropping from open mouths.

'We told a lie about where the new tomatoes came from,' says Grandpa. 'My grandson didn't really find a tomato plant in a paddock. What really happened was that I took an ordinary everyday tomato plant and did a bit of cross-pollinating in my greenhouse. Then I made up the paddock story so people would think the new tomato was natural and just as nature intended.'

The crowd has gone dead silent. All I can hear is the sound of the sea and the gulls and the gas escaping from multiple bottoms.

'We're sorry,' says Grandpa.

I nod to show I am too.

The woman from the government is looking a bit shocked. She pulls herself together and puts her hand on Grandpa's shoulder.

'We accept your apology,' she says into the microphone. 'The fact remains, you created a wonder tomato for the benefit of the world, and we want to honour you for that.'

The crowd applauds and whistles.

'Thank you,' says Grandpa. 'But there's another reason we can't accept this reward. It's hard to put into words, but every time somebody eats one of our tomatoes somewhere in the world, that's reward enough for us.'

I nod to show I agree.

The crowd is looking sort of puzzled. You know, like the eskimos when their igloos started melting and they knew they hadn't left the oven on. In social studies I wrote a letter to Iceland to say sorry, but when I showed it to Grandpa he made me tear it up, which meant I got nought out of twenty.

'I hope you understand,' Grandpa says to the crowd.

They just stare back at him.

I don't think they do.

Grandpa has been controlling himself very well so far, but now he stops clenching his buttocks and blows off big time.

I know what he's doing. Trying to give everyone a clue to help them understand.

The woman from the government is looking totally confused.

'Please,' she says. 'Just accept the honour.'

'Sorry,' says Grandpa. 'I'd rather not.'

'Me neither,' I say. 'It wouldn't be right.'

'But I don't understand,' says the woman, putting her hand over the microphone. 'You don't get any money from the tomatoes. What reward are you talking about?'

The crowd, which is frowning and muttering and giving off a lot of gas, obviously doesn't understand either.

I feel sick with nerves, but I take the microphone to explain to them.

'Our reward,' I say, 'is that our tomatoes make people fart.'

Some people in the crowd look shocked. But only because I used a rude word. They still don't get it.

Before I can continue, Grandpa takes the microphone from me and switches it off.

'Careful, Dougie,' he murmurs.

At first I think Grandpa means the rude word too. Then I realise what he's saying. We've done the right thing and confessed. No point getting ourselves in extra trouble.

'It's OK, Grandpa,' I reply quietly. 'You can trust me.'

I bite into a big red juicy tomato and sit back in my favourite chair, the cane one in Grandpa's greenhouse with the view out to sea.

I blow off, a long slow one that fills the greenhouse with a sweet tomatoey smell.

Grandpa doesn't mind. He's sitting next to me in his favourite chair doing the same.

He points down the hill towards the surf club.

'They're nearly finished,' he says.

He's right. The painters working on the Big Tomato have nearly finished painting it white.

'That was a clever idea of your mum and dad's,' says Grandpa. 'Turning it into the Big Golf Ball. When you've got the biggest caravan park in Australia, adding a beachside golf course is a top idea.'

Grandpa is right, it was a top idea. And a kind one.

A lot of the city folk in the caravan park need cheering up. It can't be easy, living in your four-wheel drive and spending all your time staring miserably at the sea and thinking about the place you used to live in that's now under water. Perhaps a bit of golf will help them feel better.

I hope so.

Grandpa has stood up and is pottering about up the other end of the greenhouse, watering his special plants. The onion weed and the kelp and the soy bean bushes and all the others. The ones he cross-pollinated with the tomato plants to get the side-effect he was after.

Grandpa's quite old and old people like to keep things for nostalgia. I'm young, but I know how he feels. We owe a lot to those plants.

Grandpa sits back down.

'Talking of clever ideas,' he says. 'Remember five years ago when the sea was still a hundred kilometres away and it didn't look like it'd ever reach us and all we had here was a drought-struck town full of dead sheep and unemployed people?'

I nod.

I'll never forget it.

Mum and Dad didn't have a job for the first six years of my life.

Grandpa's getting that misty far-away look in his eyes that old people get when they're having happy memories.

'Remember the day you asked me why the sea wasn't coming here any more?' says Grandpa. 'And I explained the ice had stopped melting because global warming was slowing down. Coal was running out and petrol was scarce and electricity was very expensive and people weren't making so much greenhouse gas and ... what was it you said?'

When Grandpa's having these memories he likes me to say exactly the same words I said five years ago.

I don't mind. I know them off by heart.

'You've got a greenhouse, Grandpa,' I recite. 'Why don't you make some greenhouse gas?'

Grandpa stares out to sea with a big smile on his face and I know what he's thinking.

About the millions of people all over the world who've been eating our tomatoes for the last five years and blowing off.

I smile too because I know what he's going to say next and it always makes me feel happy. Even being Young Australian Of The Year wouldn't make me feel happier. The only time I feel happier is when I see Mum and Dad busy and content in their caravan park by the sea.

'That greenhouse gas idea was brilliant, Dougie,' says Grandpa. 'Twenty out of twenty.'

# Think Big

## MY SCIENCE PROJECT
### BY
### TRACY SPICER
### 6W, ORCHID COVE PUBLIC SCHOOL,
### NORTH QUEENSLAND, AUSTRALIA, THE WORLD,
### THE SOLAR SYSTEM, THE MILKY WAY GALAXY,
### THE VIRGO SUPERCLUSTER, POSTCODE 4879.

## PURPOSE

The purpose of this science project is to collect data,
do research, carry out an experiment, and with a bit
of luck get Mum off that dopey diet Aunty Bev has
got her on.

## INTRODUCTION

Things are really crook. Mum's gone mental about

43

food. She reckons everything goes to her thighs. Even fish fingers. I tried to explain scientifically that's bull. Food goes to your tummy, then your bum tube. But Mum won't listen and I'm desperate. I haven't had chips for weeks. Mum steams everything. Even fish fingers.

I asked Dad to help me with the project. But he reckons getting people to do your homework is dishonest and could lead to a life of crime. It's OK for him, he goes fishing every night after work, then has a fry-up in the shed. He does offer to share his fish with me, but I can't eat them because of the tiny bones. Is there a biological reason why fish can't have drumsticks?

Anyway, I kept on at Dad about helping me. I read somewhere that a good scientist never takes no for an answer. Finally Dad blew his top and told me the scientific reason why he doesn't want to help. He hates taking sides between me and Mum. He reckons he'd rather suck snake venom out of Doug Walcott's big toe. Which he did once, so I suppose he knows what he's talking about.

## DATA COLLECTED SO FAR

1. When your Dad calms down and gives you a hug, it feels really good. Even when he's on the way to the shed and he's got a coral trout inside his shirt.

2. Mum will never be as thin as Aunty Bev. It's not scientifically possible. Aunty Bev has worn skin-tight pink jeans all her life and they've stopped her leg flesh from spreading. Plus she does that trick supermodels do. You know, wears really big dangly plastic earrings to make her body look smaller.

3. Aunty Bev has started a local Weightwatchers group. Except Weightwatchers won't let her use their name because she swore at them on the phone. So she's calling her group Think Small. It meets at our place on Thursday nights after that show on telly about fat people.

4. Mum doesn't want to be on a diet. Most of the time these days her face is longer than a school term. Plus she's got chocolate fingers hidden in her bra drawer. Aunty Bev is making Mum starve herself. She's Mum's big sister measured in years, but she's always nagging Mum about Mum being the one who's bigger measured in fat globules.

5. I hate seeing Mum unhappy.

6. I'm also worried that Mum might want us to move away. Up here in the tropics 99.999% of people wear shorts and t-shirts so your body can breathe. (The other 0.001% of people wear skin-tight pink jeans.) Now that Mum thinks she's fat she'll probably want us all to move to some

cold place where people cover up with heaps of clothes. My friend Keith lives in England and some days it's so cold there he wears three pairs of jeans. Under his school pants.

7.  Dad reckons Mum's fatness is all in her head and I think he's right. Mum is actually quite small if you compare her to the average height for a human. And her average weight is definitely not heavier than average. It's not Mum's fault she's deluded and obsessed. Aunty Bev can be harder to shake off than stringy snot. Which is why I'm using science to help Mum see the truth.

## RESEARCH METHOD

My research method consists of lying on the back lawn looking up at the stars and having dinner. I do that a lot. I love outer space. Plus Mum can't see what I'm eating. Aunty Bev can if she's got a torch.

I started my research with a research question like you're meant to. My research question was, *If Aunty Bev has her way and nobody in our family ever gets to eat another sausage and onion sandwich after the one I'm eating now, how will we cope?*

Sometimes research questions can make scientists feel a bit upset and they have to gather more data till they feel better.

I started gathering data about stars and planets. By counting them. Except as every scientist and person lying in a backyard knows, there are too many to count completely. But it does calm you down and help your digestion. It also helps you have a ripper of an idea for an experiment.

## THE EXPERIMENT
A scientific method of demonstrating to a non-fat mother who's gone a bit mental that she is not too big in any way, shape or size.

## THINGS YOU NEED TO DO THE EXPERIMENT
1. Birthday money (all of it).

2. Both of Mum's large shopping bags.

3. Fast walking to the supermarket and back so nobody notices you're gone.

4. Hiding place for the shopping bags as soon as you get home.

5. Big bone to distract Buster so he doesn't find the shopping bags behind the sofa and eat what's in them. He's got a few bits missing (one leg, half an ear, some of his tail), but that doesn't mean he's slow. His nose works super well, specially when there are large amounts of lollies in the house.

## EXPERIMENT METHOD

A laboratory wasn't available for this experiment so I used our lounge room which was better because that's where the Think Small lot were meeting.

I waited till they'd started, then walked in. Mum was there, and Aunty Bev, and Mrs Newman from the post office, and Mrs Newman's daughter Gail who works at KFC, and Doug Walcott who's been depressed and off his lollies since the snakebite. All lollies, not just jelly snakes. His wife reckons he's already lost weight. Aunty Bev doesn't. She reckons he's still pretty porky.

I asked if I could join in. Mum looked doubtful, but Aunty Bev beamed like big plastic earrings were on special and said I could as long as I waited my turn.

Mrs Newman finished telling the others her Think Small Experience Of The Week. It was about how if you steam snow peas for too long they go mushy and you don't want to eat them and you go even thinner.

The others came out with their Think Small Experiences. Each one was about not eating something or else chewing it nine million times. Everybody in that room must have been starving.

Then it was my turn.

'Trace, do you have a Think Small Experience?' said Aunty Bev. I nodded and dragged the shopping bags out from behind the sofa.

'Behold,' I said, which I think is a scientific word. 'The Milky Way.'

I ripped open a bulk bag of chocolate peanuts and tipped them on the floor. I didn't use real Milky Ways because they're the wrong shape.

Everyone stared. Not at me, at the chocolate peanuts rolling across the carpet.

'Imagine those are planets in space,' I said.

I emptied out another bag of chocolate peanuts and then lots of bags of chocolate sultanas, chocolate macadamias and chocolate hundreds and thousands.

'Our galaxy's got even more planets than that,' I said, once the floor was covered. 'There are loads we can't even see.'

Mrs Newman bent forward and peered under the coffee table. I opened a big tin of drinking chocolate powder and tipped it onto the carpet. Mum gave a kind of squeak, which I hoped showed she was getting my drift.

'Each grain of chocolate,' I said, 'is a planet in our galaxy too.'

Mrs Newman's mouth was moving silently like she was praying. Or eating. I don't think she was thinking about steamed snow peas, though. Doug Walcott's eyes were bigger than really swollen big toes. (I've never seen any, but Dad told me.) Aunty Bev was standing up, furious, looking like she was gunna do me.

I had to move quickly. I pointed to all the chocolate planets on the floor.

'Our whole galaxy,' I said, 'is in a cluster with hundreds of other galaxies.'

I held up a piece of chocolate nut cluster to illustrate the point.

'There are thousands of galaxy clusters in the universe,' I said, chucking fistfuls of chocolate nut clusters into the air. 'And there are even clusters of galaxy clusters.'

Before I could get on to how they're called superclusters and there are ten million of them in the universe, Aunty Bev grabbed me. She didn't look as amazed as I'd hoped she would. I could see I had to finish the experiment fast.

I looked around at the other stunned faces in the room. Then I concentrated all my look on Mum.

'Millions of planets in millions of galaxies in millions of superclusters,' I said to her. 'Makes you feel really small, doesn't it.'

**RESULTS**

1. I got sent to bed.

2. After the others had gone, Mum spent ages out the back staring up at the stars and planets. Dad

was with her. I peeked and saw them. Then they went into the shed.

3. Next morning all my chocolate planets and galaxies had vanished. I didn't ask Mum where they were and she didn't say.

4. I felt a bit depressed. What if the experiment had been a flop? I needed chocolate to give me hope. But there weren't even any asteroids under the coffee table.

5. I needn't have worried. That night me and Mum and Dad all had dinner together in the kitchen. Sausage and onion sandwiches. Even the bread was fried. And chocolate nut clusters for dessert. It was out of this world.

**CONCLUSION**

Science is really good, and I'm not just saying that to suck. Next project I'm going to attempt an even harder experiment. See if I can get Aunty Bev into shorts.

# Odd Socques

Macques was dreading the spelling test.
The minute he walked into class and saw the
substitute teacher sitting at Ms Conway's desk, he
knew there'd be one.

Substitute teachers always did spelling tests.

'Good morning 6C,' said the substitute teacher.
'Ms Conway is away today. My name's Mr Green.'

Macques could see something bulging in Mr
Green's jacket pocket.

Spelling test prizes.

'Good morning, Mr Green,' chanted the class.

'OK, 6C,' said Mr Green. 'I've heard you're very
good at maths and spelling. Would you rather have
a maths test or a spelling test?'

Macques sighed gloomily.

He knew exactly what was coming.

'Spelling,' yelled the class.

Mr Green looked around at all the shining

eyes and excited faces. He allowed himself a quiet smile.

A spelling class.

He'd spotted it the minute they walked in.

Then Mr Green spotted something else. A boy up the back, a boy with brown hair and a sad face, who didn't seem very delighted at all.

Can't be helped, thought Mr Green. Every class has at least one bad speller.

He pulled the bag of mini chocolate bars from his jacket pocket and waited for the cheer a teacher with lollies always got.

It didn't happen.

Mr Green looked around the class, surprised.

'A mini chocolate bar for every word you get right,' he said, in case this lot were a bit slow and didn't get how substitute teacher spelling tests worked.

Still no cheer.

Mr Green felt a moment of panic.

But only a moment. The class were still looking excited and enthusiastic. Eyes still gleaming and lots of smiles. Except the boy up the back.

How unusual, thought Mr Green. This lot seem to like spelling tests more than they like lollies.

He decided to keep the words simple, in case he was right the first time and they were a bit slow.

'OK,' he said. 'First word. Pivot. Hands up.'

Hands shot up.

Mr Green chose a girl at the front.

'P-I-V-O-T,' said Jane Dillon.

'Good,' said Mr Green and tossed her a chocolate. 'Next word, diesel.'

Sam Webster got it right.

Over the next few minutes the class also got snail, patch, gravity, blood, digital, drought, tickle and splash.

Macques wasn't surprised. He knew from experience the class were good spellers.

They'll probably get every single one, he thought gloomily. Until Mr Green asks them the one they're waiting for.

Which, a few minutes later, Mr Green did.

'Fax,' he said, taking another mini chocolate bar from the bag. 'Listen carefully. Not facts, fax.'

Every hand in the room shot up. Except Macques's.

Mr Green pointed to Tina Walsh.

'F-A-C-Q-U-E-S,' said Tina.

Mr Green looked at her, his hand frozen in mid-toss, the mini chocolate bar still between his fingers.

Strange, he thought. I wasn't told about any special needs students in this class. Perhaps she's just a comedian.

He gave her a quick frown, then pointed to the boy next to her.

'You have a go,' he said. 'Fax.'

'F-A-C-Q-U-E-S,' said Garth Spence.

Mr Green felt his face going hot.

OK, he knew what this was. Not a spelling test. A substitute teacher test.

Mr Green took a deep breath. He prided himself on always passing such tests. Well, almost always. There was the one unfortunate incident when he'd shouted at a boy for several minutes from a distance of about three centimetres, but that was months ago.

Mr Green unwrapped the untossed chocolate bar, popped it into his mouth and savoured it like he was at a wine tasting.

This didn't get the laugh he'd hoped for, but at least he was showing them he was in control.

'Let me help you,' he said to the class. 'Here's another word very similar to fax. Sax. It's short for saxaphone, my favourite musical instrument. Any jazz fans here?'

Everybody put their hands up, except the sad boy.

Mr Green had a feeling this class probably weren't jazz fans, but he pressed on.

'You,' he said, pointing to a girl. 'The word is sax.'

'S-A-C-Q-U-E-S,' said Lilly Potter.

Mr Green hestitated, not sure what to do next.

Move on to 'tax', or a maths test?

'Sir,' said a boy at the front. 'There is one person in the class who might know. His name is . . .'

The boy was trying not to giggle and he spluttered the name as he said it, but Mr Green was pretty sure it was 'Max'.

Mr Green smiled to himself. Perhaps this was a trap, perhaps it wasn't. Either way he'd win. Always easier to punish one ringleader than a whole class.

'Thank you,' he said to the boy at the front. 'Max, where are you? Stand up please.'

Slowly Macques stood up.

He didn't try to explain. He'd tried with too many other substitute teachers and he always got the blame anyway.

He knew the rest of the class were watching him. He knew they were struggling not to laugh. They always preferred to do their laughing a bit later, after the substitute teacher had got angry.

'Max,' said Mr Green. 'Spell your name for us please.'

'M-A-C-Q-U-E-S,' said Macques, wishing for the millionth time in his life that his parents hadn't done this to him.

As usual, Macques walked home from school on his own.

Near the corner of his street he heard somebody running up behind him.

Macques told himself to relax. He reminded himself that the bullying almost never happened this close to the house. But when he turned to see who it was, he still felt a jolt of anxiety.

It was Sam Webster.

'That sucked,' said Sam. 'When that substitute teacher yelled at you. Unfair.'

Macques glanced nervously up and down the street. Sam Webster usually hung out in a gang and he didn't usually have anything to say to Macques. So why was he here now?

Macques could only think of one reason. The street sign a couple of metres away. The one showing the name of Macques's street.

Knocques Avenue.

Macques glared up at the sign like he did every afternoon. He wished he could rip it down. If only someone had done that ages ago, before its stupid spelling had inspired Mum and Dad when they were looking for baby name ideas.

But it was still there and now it was the perfect mocking spot.

Max braced himself for a mocking.

Then he saw that Sam was glancing nervously up and down the street too.

'Can you keep a secret?' muttered Sam.

Macques peered around again. He couldn't see anyone else from school lurking about. He hesitated for a moment, wondering if Sam was for real. Could you trust a kid who flicked snot at substitute teachers behind their backs?

There was a kind of haunted look on Sam's face that made Macques want to trust him.

'Yes,' said Macques quietly. 'I can keep a secret.'

'Let's keep walking,' said Sam. 'I don't want anybody to hear this.'

They walked along Macques's street.

Macques waited for Sam to speak.

Sam looked as though he was having some sort of pain, possibly in the guts. Macques wondered if Sam had an allergy to mini chocolate bars.

Poor bloke, he thought, that'd be a bit rough.

Finally Sam spoke.

'I've got a dumb name too,' he muttered.

Macques looked at Sam, surprised.

Sam wasn't a silly name, nor was Webster, so it must be a secret middle one. Parents did all sorts of bad things with middle names. The worst ones were usually from dead pop singers or footy players. Elvis and Archibald, stuff like that.

Macques waited for Sam to unburden himself.

'Sam isn't spelt S-A-M,' said Sam, staring at the footpath. 'It's spelt S-A-H-M.'

Macques looked at him, even more surprised.

'My parents didn't want me to have an ordinary name,' said Sahm gloomily. 'They wanted me to be special and different and um, what's that other thing, unique.'

Macques knew all about parents wanting that.

'But . . .' said Macques. 'How did you . . . I mean how come nobody knows? How come you don't get the same treatment as me?'

Sahm glanced up and down the street again.

'I was lucky,' he said. 'When I enrolled in school the office got it wrong. They thought S-A-H-M was a spelling mistake, so they put me down as S-A-M. My parents never found out. Nor did the other kids.

But next year we go to high school. Nobody gets that lucky twice in a row. What can I do?'

Macques thought about this.

'How come your parents haven't spotted that the school is spelling your name wrong?' he asked. 'The school sends letters home all the time.'

Sahm didn't seem to hear the question.

Macques wasn't suprised.

Sahm's face was desperate and pleading. Obviously all he could think about was avoiding six years of high school bullying and misery.

Macques knew exactly how Sahm felt.

For a few seconds Macques hesitated.

Should he tell Sahm his secret? It was risky. He hadn't told anybody his confidential plan to survive high school. If it got into the wrong hands, the whole thing would be ruined and the next six years would be as bad as the last six had been.

But Sahm needed his help.

'Listen,' said Macques quietly. 'I've been talking on a chat site to some other kids with tragic names like ours. They reckon they know people who can hack into any school computer in Australia. These people charge a lot, but I'm saving up. Once I've enrolled in high school, I'm going to chuck my student card away, pay them to hack in and change my name to the proper spelling, then get a replacement card.'

Macques realised he was out of breath, even though he and Sahm had reached Macques's front gate and had stopped walking.

Sahm's eyes were shining.

'It's two hundred dollars,' said Macques. 'Can you save that much?'

Sahm didn't reply. He stuck his hands into his pockets.

'If they do yours at the same time as mine,' said Macques, 'perhaps I can get them to charge you a cheaper price.'

Sahm still didn't say anything.

Macques understood. Sahm was probably in shock about how expensive a safe and happy high school education was these days. Macques was feeling very stressed himself. If any of the kids at school found out about this . . .

Suddenly Sahm gave a big relieved grin.

'Thanks,' he said, and slapped Macques on the back.

'Think about it,' said Macques. 'If you want to give it a go, let me know.'

'I will,' said Sahm. 'Thank you so much. You're a legend.'

For a second Macques thought his new friend was going to burst into tears. Sam was struggling to keep his face under control.

Poor bloke, thought Macques. I won't invite him in. Give him a bit of time on his own to calm himself down.

He gave Sahm a wave and headed for the front door.

On his way there, he had a nagging thought. The way Sahm had slapped him on the back. Kids at school didn't usually do that. Not unless . . .

At the front door Macques turned and glanced back at Sahm. And saw the giggling faces of the rest of the gang, crouching in the hedge.

Sahm, or rather Sam, didn't look tearful any more. He was laughing even harder than the others.

Macques managed to get the key in the lock. Inside, once the door was shut, he squeezed his eyes closed and struggled with his own tears.

Real ones.

Then he wiped his eyes and checked his back in the hall mirror. He wasn't surprised to see something stuck there.

A yellow post-it note with two words scrawled on it.

*Tricqued You.*

Macques waited until dinner time to have another go at Mum and Dad.

'Please let me change my name,' he begged. 'Please let me spell it M-A-X.'

Mum and Dad looked at each other.

They both sighed, but they didn't say anything until they'd finished chewing their mouthfuls of pan-seared swordfish with balsamic vinegar and pink peppercorns.

'Darling,' said Mum. 'We've explained this to

you so often. Macques is a lovely name. It's special and distinctive and unique. Like you.'

'Forget those pea-brains at school,' said Dad. 'Once you're out in the big wide world, you'll be glad you've got a name that people notice. In those hospitals or TV stations or nuclear research facilities or wherever you end up working, there'll be all the ordinary Maxes, but only one Macques.'

Mum and Dad both glowed.

Macques wasn't sure if it was from pride or pink peppercorns.

'I want to be an ordinary Max,' he said.

This time Mum and Dad didn't wait till they'd finished chewing.

'That is crazy talk,' said Mum. 'You are not ordinary.'

'I am,' said Macques.

'Rubbish,' said Dad. 'When you were born we decided we weren't going to let you be ordinary. That's why we didn't give you a boring ordinary name like our parents gave us.'

'Eric and Joan are nice names,' said Macques.

Mum and Dad both sighed crossly.

'When will you get it into your head?' said Dad. 'You won't stand out in the crowd if people think you're ordinary and boring.'

'Why do you think me and Dad go to so much trouble?' said Mum.

Macques knew what was coming next.

Mum swung her feet out from under the table,

pulled up the legs of her black tracksuit and pointed to her socks. One was pink, one was orange.

'I'm the only person at the gym with odd socks,' she said. 'Nobody there thinks I'm ordinary.'

Dad twanged his braces. They had green sheep on them.

'One look at my braces,' said Dad, 'and everyone in my office knows I'm not ordinary.'

'Do you see, Macques?' said Mum. 'Do you see what we're saying?'

Macques replied through gritted teeth.

'Yes,' he said. 'You're saying that the reason you drive the same foreign cars as everyone else and wear the same designer clothes as everyone else and eat the same swordfish with balsamic vinegar and pink peppercorns as everyone else is so everyone will think you're not ordinary.'

'Macques,' said Mum.

'Careful, young man,' said Dad.

'But you are ordinary,' said Macques. 'I am too.'

Macques realised he was standing up and shouting and several of his pink peppercorns were on the handwoven Icelandic tablecloth.

He didn't care.

'I just want us to be an ordinary family,' he pleaded.

'Macques,' yelled Mum. 'Stop yelling. We do not yell in this house.'

'Go to your room,' said Dad with icy calm. 'Have a long hard think. I don't want to see you or hear a peep from you until you come to your senses.'

'Nor do I,' said Mum.

Macques threw himself onto his bed and buried his face in his Scandinavian-style organic goose-down pillow.

I can't take it any more, he thought desperately.

He used to think he could.

He used to think that if he got through life one day at a time, he could make it to his eighteenth birthday and then leave home and change his name.

Not any more.

'Help,' he whispered into his pillow. 'I need help.'

Then he stopped. One thing he'd learned in life was that pillows couldn't help with the really big problems. Small ones, like being tired or having a stiff neck, yes. Big ones, like war and disease and having a stupid name, no.

The other reason Macques stopped was that somebody was tapping at his window.

He jumped up.

Even before he opened the curtain, Macques felt anger burning through him.

Sam Webster and his gang. Still loitering in the front yard. Still hoping to get a bit more taunting and mocking in before bedtime.

Thank you Sam, thought Macques grimly. You don't know it, but I'm very glad you're still here.

When I haul you in through that window and drag you down to Mum and Dad, then maybe they'll understand.

Macques flung the curtains open.

And stared.

It wasn't Sam and his mates.

Four other kids were standing outside looking at Macques through the glass. It was dark out there, but the light from the room shone on their faces. Two boys and two girls, all wearing white overalls. Macques had never seen any of them before.

One of the boys signalled to Macques to open the window.

Macques hesitated. Then he saw that the boy had a name tag on his overalls. It said *Nickless*.

Max opened the window.

'G'day,' said the boy. 'Unfair Name Rescue Squad. Are you Macques spelled M-A-C-Q-U-E-S?'

Dazed, Macques nodded.

'We're here to rescue you,' said the boy.

Macques didn't understand.

He saw that the others had name tags too. The other boy's said *Shorn*. The girls' were *Jeen* and *Kaitye*.

'Sorry we've taken a while to get to you,' said Jeen. 'Big backlog.'

'Unfair Name Rescue Squad?' said Macques.

Then he realised what was going on. It was another trick. The most complicated piece of bullying and mockery yet. These kids weren't even from his school. Somebody must have paid them.

'Do you want to be rescued?' said Kaitye.

Macques nodded.

He could see they'd even got a taxi waiting out in the street. It was perfect. He'd pretend to go along with them, and when they all got to the taxi he'd yell for Mum and Dad. Then Mum and Dad would see the sort of thing an unfair name did for you and they really would understand.

Macques opened the window wider.

'No need to bring anything,' said Shorn.

This lot are very good, thought Macques as they helped him down from the window. Perhaps they're a high school drama group.

As he hurried across the front yard with them, Macques had a thought. A quick flash of a thought that was stupid but he had it anyway because it felt so good even just for a fleeting moment.

How incredible and amazing and wonderful it would be if the Unfair Name Rescue Squad was real.

No.

Impossible.

Don't even hope.

Then Macques saw the lit-up sign on the roof of the taxi.

TACQUESI.

'Don't worry,' said Nickless, who was sitting next to Macques in the back of the taxi. 'This won't take long.'

'Only round the block,' said Jeen.

'Just as well these rescues are quick,' said Shorn from the front. 'We've got three more jobs tonight.'

Macques felt a stab of panic as they sped away down the dark street, partly because he'd always promised Mum and Dad he'd never get into a taxi with people he didn't know, and partly because Kaitye was driving and he was pretty sure she was too young to have a licence or third-party insurance.

At the top end of Macques's street they turned the corner.

'Where are you from?' asked Macques.

He wanted them to be real, he did so much, but part of his brain kept saying *TV show* and *I wonder where the camera's hidden*.

'The UNRS operates all over the world,' said Nickless. 'Thousands of us. And we're all flat out.'

'Dunno who kicked off this craze for dodgy names,' said Jeen. 'They should be locked up.'

The taxi turned another corner.

'Where are we going?' asked Macques.

'Home,' said Shorn.

'Your home,' said Kaitye.

Macques didn't understand.

'Your real home,' said Nickless.

Macques still didn't understand.

He was still trying to work out what they meant, and wondering if the TV show host was in the boot, when the taxi made the final turn of the block into the bottom end of Macques's street.

Macques knew it was his street because through the taxi window he could see the street sign, clear as anything in the light from a street lamp.

Knox Avenue.

Macques stared.

'Look,' he said. 'The spelling's changed. It's Knox, K-N-O-X.'

'That's right,' said Jeen.

Macques felt dizzy. Not in a horrible I'm-going-to-throw-up way. In a nice this-is-very-weird-but-I-don't-want-it-to-end way.

The taxi stopped outside Macques's house.

'That's it,' said Nickless. 'We're done. You're rescued.'

Nickless got out.

Macques realised he was meant to get out too, but he was finding it hard to actually move.

'Go,' said Shorn. 'We're on a schedule.'

Macques got out.

'How do I know this isn't all a dream?' he heard himself say to Nickless.

Nickless smiled and Macques had the feeling Nickless got asked that question a lot.

'How do you know all that stuff before we arrived wasn't a dream?' said Nickless.

Macques wished his thoughts weren't so scrambled. He felt like one of those characters in a science fiction movie who gets taken at warp-speed into another dimension and arrives with bulging eyes and sticking-out hair and a smoking brain.

He put his hand to his head. His hair felt fine. But then he had only been round the block.

'Hope you like your parents,' said Nickless, getting back into the taxi and pulling the door shut.

Macques wasn't sure he'd heard that right. But it was too late to check. The taxi was driving away.

He gave the Unfair Name Rescue Squad a wave and watched the lit-up sign on the top of the taxi disappear into the darkness.

TAXI, it said.

Inside the house, everything looked exactly the same.

Well, almost. The wallpaper was a bit different, and the carpet, and there was a pine dresser in the hallway Macques didn't completely remember.

Macques stared at his reflection in the hall mirror.

His face looked the same and he felt wide awake.

There was nothing stuck to his back.

'Dinner's ready,' sang out Mum's voice.

Macques went into the living room. Mum and Dad were sitting at the table. They looked exactly the same too.

Well, almost.

They both looked slightly plumper and Mum's hair was curly instead of straight.

Macques started to feel a little bit panicked.

Then he saw something that made the panic go away. The big loving smiles on Mum and Dad's faces.

'Tuck in,' said Mum.

On the table were three plates of fish and chips. Mum was already stuffing quite a few chips into her mouth at once.

'Come on,' said Dad, winking at Macques. 'Make the most of it. You'll probably only be living at home for another ten years or so. Get Mum's cooking into you while you have the chance.'

Macques did just that. It was the best fish and chips he'd ever tasted. The more chips he put into his mouth, the happier he felt.

There were lots of questions buzzing around in his head, but they could wait till later.

Except one.

After a few more mouthfuls, Macques decided to get it over with.

'Mum and Dad,' he said. 'Can you test my spelling?'

Mum and Dad looked a bit nervous.

'OK,' said Dad. 'But we're pretty ordinary spellers.'

Macques couldn't help smiling to himself. Last time he'd asked Mum and Dad for a spelling test, they'd given him words like vicissitude and extracurricular and had gone on for hours about how important a big and impressive vocabulary was.

'You give me the word,' said Macques, 'and I'll spell it.'

'OK,' said Mum.

'Start with my name,' said Macques.

'You kind thing,' said Mum. 'Letting us all kick off with an easy one.'

'OK,' said Dad. 'Here goes.'

'Max,' said Mum.

'M-A-X,' said Macques.

He held his breath.

'Correct,' said Mum and Dad, grinning at him. 'Very good.'

Max grinned back. They were right, it was very good.

As Mum leaned over and gave him a hug, Max took a peek at her socks.

Both grey.

They were ordinary and they matched.

# Ashes To Ashes

It's the last half-hour of the fifth cricket test.
I can hardly breathe.

I feel almost as woozy as poor Grandad must have felt a month ago when his insides packed up and his innings finally came to an end.

The whole Ashes test series is hanging in the balance. We've won two matches and England have won two.

This is the decider.

It'll all be over soon. England need twelve more runs and they're batting well. Australia need one more wicket and they're bowling like year threes. And I'm sitting here in the northern stand holding something that could help Australia win this match, and the whole series, and the Ashes.

I'm holding some other ashes.

Grandad's ashes.

'Whoo,' says Pino, 'Look at her.'

My friend Pino isn't interested in cricket. He's only interested in girls. He's been that way for most of year seven. He only agreed to come to the cricket today because he reckons it's a top place to meet girls who aren't your sisters or aunties.

'Nice,' says Pino, leaning forward in his seat. His eyes are so wide the green and yellow stripes on his face are going bendy.

I asked Pino to come today because he's brave and reckless. You'd have to be to talk to girls who are complete strangers. When I try and do it, my mouth stops working and my fingers go all twisted like a spin bowler's.

But I'm not here for girls today, I'm here for something much more important. That's why I asked Pino. I need his help to do something even more dangerous than talk to girls.

'That one,' says Pino, nudging me so hard I almost drop the urn. 'The one with her dad.'

I try to see who he's pointing at. I can't. There are sixty thousand people in this stadium and about six thousand of them are girls with their dads.

'If I'm not back in five minutes,' says Pino, 'tell my mum I'm getting married.'

I try to stop him. I try to remind him that his parents don't even think he's mature enough to use the slicing machine in their deli, so it's unlikely they'll agree to a wedding.

'Come with me,' says Pino. 'She might have a friend.'

I shake my head.

Even the thought of it makes my hands go all googly.

'Tragic,' says Pino, looking at me not very sympathetically.

Then he's gone.

And time's running out.

Relax, I tell myself. He'll be back soon. He's left his lollies.

England score two more runs.

I check the breeze. And nearly have a serious Grandad-sized heart failure. The wind has changed direction. It's blowing towards us now. We'll have to go all the way over to the other side of the stadium to do what we have to do.

'Don't worry, Grandad,' I whisper to the urn. 'We'll make it.'

I try to sound more confident than I feel.

Pino comes back, frowning.

'I was wrong,' he says. 'She's not very nice. Neither's her dad.'

I can see them both now. They're looking across at Pino and laughing at him in an unkind sort of way.

I should be a good friend and tell Pino that the face paint probably isn't helping, or the hanky he's got tied round his head with *England sucks* scrawled on it.

But there isn't time.

'Change of plan,' I say. 'We have to go over to the other side and scatter my grandad's ashes there.'

75

Pino stares at me.

'Why?' he says. 'Your grandad just wants to be laid to rest on hollowed turf. Why does it matter which side?'

'Hallowed,' I say. 'Test cricket turf is called hallowed.'

'Whatever,' says Pino. 'In his will your grandad just asked to be scattered on a test cricket pitch, that's what you said. He didn't mention anything about which side.'

'Actually,' I confess, 'he didn't mention anything about a test cricket pitch either. But I know it's where he'd want to be. He loved cricket even more than beer.'

I shudder as I think what Mum and Dad will do when they find that Grandad's urn isn't on the kitchen shelf any more. That's if they notice. They're probably still too busy arguing about where to scatter him.

'Look at it this way,' says Pino. 'People don't care which side of the glass they drink beer from and they don't care which side of a test cricket pitch they're scattered on. It's gunna be hard enough fighting our way onto the pitch with everyone else at the end of the match. At least over this side we're close to the fence.'

I start to explain to Pino that the plan has changed from the one I told him this morning. That we're going to do more than just lay Grandad to rest on hallowed turf. Much more. And we don't need to be near the fence to do it. The most important thing now is wind direction.

Then I stop.

We're running out of time.

'The girls over the other side might be nicer,' I say.

Pino follows me without another word.

In the tunnel that leads to the other side of the stadium, I explain the new plan.

'Scatter the ashes in the air?' says Pino. 'Why?'

'So Australia can win,' I say.

Pino looks puzzled.

We can't see the pitch, but I can hear the England supporters cheering. England must have scored more runs.

I explain the new plan in detail.

'There are millions of bits of Grandad in here,' I say, shaking the urn. 'With the wind behind them, chances are at least one of the bits will end up in an English batsman's eye.'

Pino thinks about this.

'So he can't see properly,' says Pino.

'Yes,' I say.

'So he gets bowled,' says Pino.

'Exactly,' I say.

'So Australia wins,' says Pino.

'Spot on,' I say.

He's pretty smart for someone who doesn't know much about cricket.

'That is so stupid,' says Pino.

I look at him.

Smart, but not very confident about the future.

I think it must come from talking to girls.

When we hurry out of the tunnel I look across at the scoreboard.

England only need six more runs.

'Come on,' I say to Pino. We run up the steps.

I reckon the highest part of the stadium will be the best place for scattering ashes. I can see big sliding windows behind the back row of seats. They're open for ventilation, and a strong breeze is blowing through them and gusting towards us as we climb higher.

'Anyway,' pants Pino. 'Why would your grandad want Australia to win? He was from England, wasn't he? That's like my dad wanting Italy to lose at soccer. My whole family would put their heads in the meat slicer before they'd want that.'

I explain about Grandad.

'He wanted England to lose at everything,' I say. 'He hated the place because he had such an unhappy childhood there. His parents were very strict. He got bullied a lot by other boys. Girls thought he was a nerd.'

'Sounds pretty normal,' mutters Pino.

More applause from parts of the crowd. England have scored two more runs.

We reach the back row of seats.

'Right,' I say to Pino. 'Go over there and do

something that'll make everybody look at you.'

Pino hesitates, uncertain.

'People mustn't see me scattering Grandad,' I say. 'It's a serious crime, temporarily blinding a tail-ender batsman.'

Pino thinks about this.

'OK,' he says. 'But if you get arrested, I'll have to pretend I don't know you. Or your grandad.'

'Of course,' I say quietly.

Pino goes along behind the seats.

Clutching Grandad to my chest, I loosen the lid of the urn and unscrew it with as little movement as possible and slip the lid into my back pocket.

'What have you got there?' says a voice.

I try and stuff Grandad out of sight as well, but my t-shirt's not baggy enough.

'We did that once,' says the voice.

It's a girl.

She's about my age and she's sitting at the end of the back row, staring at the urn and grinning.

I try to control my panic. I also try to remember if Australia has won any other test series because a tail-ender batsman got something in his eye.

'Our cat Warnie died,' says the girl. 'He loved cricket, but he'd only ever seen it on telly, so we brought his ashes here for a first-hand squiz.'

I don't know what to say. It's the same as always. Whenever I try to have a conversation with a girl, my brain feels like Ricky Ponting has whacked it with his bat. Must be a gene I inherited from

Grandad. The nerd gene. Actually I think I'm even more of a nerd than he was. At least Grandad ended up married. I'm probably going to end up on my own, babysitting Pino's kids.

'Pretty funny, eh,' says the girl, still looking up at me. 'Bringing ashes to see who wins the Ashes.'

She's got the friendliest grin I've ever seen.

I open my mouth, trying to think of something to say to her that can't be used against me later in court.

Before I can speak, a commotion starts up further along the row of seats. It's Pino, yelling and clapping.

'England sucks,' he chants. 'England sucks, England sucks, England sucks.'

Everyone, including the girl, turns to look at him.

I don't waste a second.

'Bye, Grandad,' I whisper.

I grip Grandad in both hands and swing the urn in a big movement so all his ashes fly out into the wind. Which, I realise too late, isn't blowing towards the pitch any more. It's changed direction again. It's blowing towards me, and towards the huge ventilation windows behind me.

Grandad swirls around the back of the stand for a few seconds, then disappears out through the windows.

Frantic, I dive after him, but it's too late.

I stick my head through one of the open windows.

I can just make out the dusty cloud that is Grandad, getting fainter by the second as he's blown down into the busy street below.

He's being scattered among people who don't even know he's there. People getting on with their busy lives. Squabbling about parking spaces. Laughing at other people who've dropped their shopping. Walking past a charity collector and ignoring her.

I can see bits of Grandad landing on a mother who is smacking her crying toddler. And on several big kids who are chasing after a small kid.

Instead of laying Grandad to rest on hallowed turf, I've dumped him in the middle of people doing nasty things.

Things that aren't cricket.

Suddenly, behind me, the crowd roars and groans all at once.

I turn round.

England have scored a boundary.

Four runs.

Both English batsmen are standing with their arms in the air. Our players have slumped. Some are crouching with their heads in their hands. Others are sitting dejectedly on the grass as if they've just tried to talk to a girl and been laughed at.

We've lost.

England have won the match. And the whole test series. And the Ashes.

I turn back to the window. I can't even see

Grandad down in the street now. Not one single tiny bit of him.

'Well,' says Pino, coming over. 'That was successful.'

'Sorry, Grandad,' I whisper.

We head towards the exit. Most of the departing crowd are looking unhappy. I bet they don't feel as unhappy as me.

Losing a test series is bad, but not as bad as what I've done.

Pino isn't looking happy either. There were groups of England fans up the back of the stand when he was chanting, and he's worried about what they'll do to him if they see him. He's taken his *England Sucks* hanky off and stuffed it in his pocket.

We're in the street now.

I look down, just in case there are any specks of Grandad on the footpath. It's no good, my eyesight isn't strong enough. Anyway, even if I did see some bits of ash, how would I know it was Grandad and not the remains of a cigarette or a cricket-loving cat?

'Sorry, Grandad,' I whisper again. 'Sorry you ended up somewhere you didn't want to be.'

Grandad always hated crowded streets. He was always worried someone would jostle him and he'd drop his shopping. And if someone squabbled with him about a parking spot, he'd always give in.

I look up from the footpath.

All around me, people are rubbing their eyes.

The mother who was smacking the toddler is rubbing hers while the toddler chuckles happily.

The big kids who were chasing the small kid are rubbing theirs while the small kid disappears into a side street.

The people who were laughing at the dropped shopping are rubbing theirs with both hands. One of them is dropping his shopping while he does it.

This is weird.

I should be feeling guilty, but instead I'm getting a strange feeling. A feeling that this is where Grandad wants to be. I can't explain it. But the more I look around, the stronger I feel it.

Then I see something else.

'Look,' I say.

Pino ducks behind a bus shelter. He thinks I've seen some England fans. But that's not what I'm pointing at.

It's the girl from the back row of the stand. She's with a man who's bent forward with his hands over his eyes.

'Careful, Dad,' she says. 'Let me try and get it out.'

'Gently, love,' he replies. 'It feels like grit.'

Before I have a chance to think what I'm doing, I grab the hanky from Pino's pocket, lick the corner and go over to the girl and her father.

'Um,' I say. 'Excuse me. My dad's a demolition contractor and he works with dust all the time. This is something my grandad taught us.'

I gently hold one of the father's eyes open with my thumb and forefinger, and dab away the tears with Pino's hanky. A bit of the marker pen Pino used for the writing gets on the father's eye socket, but I'm sure he won't mind.

With the corner of the hanky I flick a couple of bits of Grandad out of the father's eye. Then I do the other side.

Once the girl's father can see again, he gives me a grateful look.

'Thank you very much, young man,' he says.

Oh no. Now he's peering at me as if he's seen me before but he's not sure where.

I hope the girl won't tell him. I hope she won't say anything about bringing ashes to the Ashes and unpredictable wind changes. If the people in this street hear, they'll lynch me.

She doesn't.

'Thanks,' she says to me, grinning again. Then she steps very close and murmurs something else. 'Next time you bring a member of your family to the cricket, give the rest of us some warning, OK?'

'OK,' I say.

She turns to Pino, who's staring at us both, stunned.

'What's your friend's name?' she asks him.

'Um . . .' he says.

'Mark Smalley,' I say, amazed how easily the words come out.

'I'm Alice,' says the girl.

'G'day Alice,' I say.

'Well, Mark,' says Alice's father. 'If you end up being an eye doctor, let us know. We'll be your first clients.'

'Actually,' I say, 'I'm planning on being a Porsche dealer. Or a test cricketer.'

Alice doesn't laugh, or mock, or chuck me one of those 'as if' looks. She just gives me another friendly smile.

'See you around,' she says, and I can see she means it.

'Thanks again,' says her father.

'Nice to meet you,' I say as they head into the crowd.

Pino seems to have lost the power of speech.

I, on the other hand, suddenly feel like I could rabbit on till midnight. With Alice or any one of the other five thousand nine hundred and ninety-nine girls leaving the cricket stadium.

But I don't. What I want to say only needs two words.

'Thanks, Grandad,' I whisper.

# 101 Text Messages
# You Must Read
# Before You Die

DEAR RO HERE IT IS MY FIRST ONE WITHOUT
YOUR HELP PRETTY GOOD EH JEEZ FINDING THE
LETTERS TAKES AGES ANYWAY MY TEXT MESSAGE
IS CAN I HAVE A CUP OF TEA PLEASE
LOVE DAD

RO ARE YOU THERE

DAD TO RO BUNG THE KETTLE ON

COME ON RO ITS THIRSTY WORK HERE IN THE
ORCHARD NOW WEVE DECIDED TO GO ORGANIC
AND STOP USING SPRAYS AND I HAVE TO YELL AT
THE BUGS TO GET OFF THE APPLES

RO WAKE UP IM DRYER THAN A WALLABYS
WASHING

OOPS DOPEY ME YOU CANT READ THIS IF YOURE
STILL ASLEEP AND I DONT BLAME YOU IF YOU ARE
AFTER WHAT THOSE CHEESE BRAINS DID TO YOU AT
SCHOOL LAST NIGHT

DONT WORRY LOVE IM COMING UP TO THE HOUSE

GET OFF THAT APPLE YOU MONGREL

SORRY RO NOT YOU

OOPS JUST REMEMBERED WHAT YOU TOLD ME
ABOUT KEEPING THE WORDS SHORT IN TXTS

TRBLE IS WHN I DO I CANT UNDRSTND WHT IM
SAYNG ITS A CMPLT MNGRL

BACK TO BIG WORDS NO SWEAT IVE GOT STRONG
THUMBS I CAN HANDLE IT I DONT KNOW HOW YOU
KIDS CAN UNDERSTAND ABBRV ABBRIV SHORT
WORDS

HEY IM GETTING FASTER AT THIS ALMOST AT
THE HOUSE NOW IGNORE THIS IF YOURE STILL
SNOOZING

YOURE NOT STILL SNOOZING WHERE ARE YOU LOVE
YOUR BEDS EMPTY AND SO ARE YOUR JARMIES AND
YOURE NOT IN THE SHOWER OR THE KITCHEN OR
THE HALL CUPBOARD

I BET YOURE UP THE BACK PADDOCK GIVING THE
LONG GRASS A WALLOPING AND PRETENDING
ITS MR CHEESE BRAIN GLOSSOP GOOD GIRL HE
DESERVES TO HAVE HIS EDGES TRIMMED AFTER
WHAT HE DID TO US LAST NIGHT

THE MONGREL

THIS CROOK MOBILE RECEPTION IN THE BUSH
IS A PAIN IN THE APPLES I MEAN IF A BLOKE
WANTS TO RING UP HIS DAUGHTER BY VOICE
TO SEE IF SHES OK HE CANT YEAH I KNOW TEXTS
ARE BEST FOR YOU RO BUT IT STILL GETS UP MY
NOSE

GIVE THAT BACK PADDOCK AN EXTRA WHACK FROM
ME LOVE BUT SEND ME A TEXT FIRST SO I KNOW
YOURE OK

HANG ON IM UP ON THE ROOF NOW AND I CAN SEE
THE BACK PADDOCK AND YOURE NOT THERE

ALSO YOURE NOT IN THE FRONT PADDOCK OR THE
SIDE PADDOCK OR THE PACKING SHED

OH NO THE TRACTOR ISNT IN THE PACKING SHED
EITHER

RO URGENT URGENT URGENT WHEREVER YOU ARE
STOP DRIVING THE TRACTOR NOW AND TURN THE
ENGINE OFF COMPLETELY AND GET AWAY FROM IT
I KNOW YOURE ALLOWED TO DRIVE IT BUT THIS IS
DIFFERENT SEE NEXT MESSAGE

DANGER FUEL TANK LEAKING

ITS FROM WHEN I ACCIDENTLY BACKED INTO THAT
FOOTY CLUB BUS AFTER THEY LAUGHED AT YOU FOR
SPEAKING WITH YOUR HANDS

OK I SHOULD HAVE GOT IT FIXED BUT I HAVENT HAD
TIME WHAT WITH HELPING YOU PRACTISE FOR THE
SCHOOL DEBATE AND LEARNING ORGANIC APPLE
GROWING METHODS SO I PATCHED IT UP BUT IF THE
CHEWY GIVES WAY IT COULD BE A BIT DANGEROUS

VERY DANGEROUS

THE TRACTOR COULD BLOW UP LOVE

TURN THE ENGINE OFF NOW RO OH JEEZ WHY
ARENT YOU ANSWERING MY MESSAGES

IM ON THE GROUND WITH MY EAR IN THE DIRT
TRYING TO HEAR WHICH DIRECTION YOUVE GONE
BUT I CANT HEAR ANY ENGINE VIBRATIONS CAUSE
THE GRASSHOPPERS ARE TOO LOUD

IF YOUVE TAKEN THE TRACTOR OVER TO NEXT
DOORS ORCHARD TO PULL SCARY FACES AT THEIR
INSECTS I WONT BE CROSS

RO TALK TO ME TELL ME WHERE YOU ARE TELL ME
YOUVE DITCHED THE TRACTOR PLEASE

IM RUSHING ROUND THE HOUSE LIKE A MANIAC
SEEING IF YOU LEFT A NOTE BUT THERE ISNT ONE IN
THE KITCHEN OR THE LOUNGE OR TIED TO THE DOG
WHY DO YOU CHOOSE A DIFFERENT PLACE EACH
TIME

FOUND IT I SHOULD HAVE LOOKED ON THE TOILET
DOOR FIRST OFF OK LETS SEE WHERE YOU ARE

OH JEEZ RO NO NO NO TAKING THE TRACTOR TO
TOWN IS TOO FAR LISTEN ITS A BIT TECHNICAL BUT
IF THE CHEWY OVERHEATS AND FUEL SPLASHES
ONTO THE INTAKE MANIFOLD YOURE HISTORY

IM IN THE TRUCK IM COMING AFTER YOU

NO IM NOT THE TRUCK WONT START

IM SURE I PUT THOSE NEW SPARK PLUGS IN THE
BATHROOM CABINET DID YOU MOVE THEM

FOUND THEM MY FAULT THEY WERE IN MY SOCK
DRAWER

IM COMING AFTER YOU YOUR TYRE TRACKS IN THE
DRIVEWAY LOOK FRESH SO I HOPE YOURE NOT TOO
FAR AHEAD STOP DRIVING RO PLEASE

WICH WAY DID YOU GO MAIN ROAD OR BAK WAY
SORRY ABOUT THE SPELING IM TEXTING ONE
HANDED I REKON THE BAC WAY CAUSE YOUR A KID
AND KIDS DRIVING TRACTRS ON MAIN RODS STIK
OUT LIKE MOTHS BALLS

THATS BETTER STEERING WITH MY KNEES NOW
BOTH HANDS FOR TEXTING RO ANSWER ME BUT
FIRST PLEASE STOP THE TRACTOR AND RUN

OH NO ITS JUST HIT ME WHY YOURE NOT
ANSWERING AND WHY YOU DON'T WANT TO STOP
DRIVING INTO TOWN

REVENGE

LISTEN RO I AGREE WHAT THAT CHEESE BRAIN
GLOSSOP DID LAST NIGHT WAS A CROOK THING

I DONT MEAN SNEERING AT MY ORANGE AND
PURPLE COWBOY SHIRT I MEAN CHUCKING A
BRILLIANT DEBATER OFF THE TEAM JUST CAUSE SHE
WAS BORN WITH HER VOICE MISSING AND SHE HAS
TO DEBATE WITH HER HANDS

IT WASNT YOUR FAULT THAT AMANDA WAS BEING
REALLY SLOW TELLING THE OTHER TEAM WHAT YOU
WERE SAYING SO I HAD TO HELP OUT

OK I WAS A BIT LOUD AT FIRST BUT THATS CAUSE I
WAS STANDING UP THE BACK OF THE HALL

I WAS ONLY TRYING TO HELP

WHERE ARE YOU RO STOP THE TRACTOR PLEASE

I CANT STAND THIS EVERY TIME I GO ROUND A
CORNER I THINK IM GUNNA SEE A BIG CLOUD OF
SMOKE AND A BLOWN UP TRACTOR AND A BLOWN
UP DAUGHTER

OK I DID GET A BIT CARRIED AWAY LAST NIGHT BUT
ONLY BECAUSE OF THE DEBATING TOPIC

WHAT SORT OF DEBATING TOPIC IS WORDS SPEAK
LOUDER THAN ACTIONS

WHAT AN INSULT

THERE YOU WERE SITTING ON THAT STAGE A TOP
LIVING BREATHING EXAMPLE OF HOW ACTIONS
ALWAYS SPEAK LOUDER THAN WORDS AND THEY
STILL RECKONED THEY HAD TO DEBATE IT

SO I SAW RED APPLES AND DID SOME THINGS
I SHOULDNT HAVE

ITS LIKE CARLA TAMWORTH SAYS IN HER CLASSIC
SONG ABOUT THE BLOKE WHO DOESNT WANT TO
ADMIT HES GOT A BOIL ON HIS BUM SO HE SITS ALL
DAY ON HIS HORSE IN AGONY

YOUVE GOT TO STAND UP FOR THE TRUTH

ID SING IT TO YOU IF YOU WERE HERE JEEZ YOU
MUST BE A LONG WAY IN FRONT IM DRIVING LIKE
A MANIAC

NO IM NOT RO DONT WORRY IVE GOT VERY SAFE
KNEES

PLEASE RO WHY DONT YOU STOP AND TURN THE
TRACTOR OFF AND LET ME CATCH UP WITH YOU SO
I CAN APOLOGISE

IM SORRY I WENT UP ON STAGE LAST NIGHT AND
MUCKED UP THE DEBATE

I JUST WANTED TO MAKE SURE THEY GOT THAT
BRILLIANT THING YOU SAID ABOUT ACTIONS
SPEAKING LOUDER THAN WORDS EG PARENTS WHO
MIME COUNTRY AND WESTERN SONGS TO THEIR
KIDS IN THE BATH

THAT WAS ONE OF THE BEST DEBATING ARGUMENTS
IVE EVER HEARD AND THE ONLY REASON I SANG AT
THAT POINT WAS TO GIVE THEM AN EXAMPLE

I WOULD HAVE NICKED OFF THEN LIKE MR GLOSSOP
TOLD ME TO IF THAT CAPTAIN OF THE OTHER TEAM
HADNT GOT PERSONAL

WHEN HE SAID AN EXAMPLE OF WORDS SPEAKING
LOUDER THAN ACTIONS WAS PEOPLE WHO WORE
DUMB BELT BUCKLES WITH THE WORDS LOVE AND
DEATH ON THEM EVERYBODY IN THAT HALL KNEW
HE WAS TALKING ABOUT ME BECAUSE GLOSSOP
WAS WEARING BRACES

AS YOU KNOW I BOUGHT THAT SKELETON ON A
HARLEY BUCKLE TO WEAR AT YOUR MUMS FUNERAL
AND ITS VERY PRECIOUS TO ME SO I HAD TO
DEBATE HIM BACK

IM SORRY IT GOT US CHUCKED OUT AND IM SORRY
I SAID THAT STUPID THING DRIVING HOME ABOUT
HOW SOMEONE SHOULD TOW GLOSSOPS FLASH
NEW CAR INTO THE RIVER

I SHOULD NEVER HAVE SAID THOSE WORDS IN
FRONT OF A PERSON WHOS SO TOP AT DOING
ACTIONS

DONT DO IT RO IF YOU TRY AND TOW ANYTHING
WITH THAT TRACTOR YOULL OVERSTRESS THE
CHEWY

OH JEEZ IF THE TRACTOR BLOWS UP ILL NEVER
FORGIVE MYSELF

WHERE ARE YOU LOVE I DONT GET IT IM PULLING
INTO TOWN NOW AND THERES NO SIGN OF YOU.

DID I PASS YOU IN A DUST CLOUD ON THE DIRT
TRACK AND NOT SEE YOU CAUSE THE TRACTOR HAD
ALREADY BLOWN UP AND ALL THE BITS OF YOU ON
THE ROAD WERE TOO SMALL

OH NO

BLACK SMOKE

DIRECTLY OVER THE SCHOOL CARPARK

NO PLEASE NO IF YOURE STILL ALIVE LOVE JUST LIE
STILL DONT TRY TO MOVE IM GETTING TO YOU AS
FAST AS I CAN

WHY DO PEOPLE HAVE SO MUCH GARDEN
FURNITURE IT MAKES THEIR BACKYARDS REALLY
HARD TO DRIVE THROUGH

HANG ON RO

HOW OFTEN AT P AND C MEETINGS HAVE I SAID THE
SCHOOL CARPARK NEEDS A BACK ENTRANCE NOW
ILL HAVE TO DRIVE THROUGH THE PETROL STATION
FENCE

OUCH ITS OK IM NOT HURT

SHOULD HAVE LOOSENED MY BELT BUCKLE BEFORE
THE IMPACT BUT ITS ONLY A FLESH WOUND

SMOKE EVERYWHERE NOW

RO WHERE ARE YOU

I CANT LOOK DON'T BE DEAD

WHAT HAVE I DONE

EVERYTHING I DO IS TO TRY AND PROTECT YOU
THATS THE ONLY REASON I STOPPED THE SPRAYING
PLUS AS YOU CORRECTLY POINTED OUT WHEN THE
WIND BLOWS THE SPRAY ONTO THE WASHING IT
ROTS THE ELASTIC IN MY UNDIES

BE ALIVE RO PLEASE

I WANT TO HAVE LOTS MORE DEBATES WITH YOU
ABOUT WHETHER ORANGE GOES WITH PURPLE
AND THE BEST RECIPE FOR APPLE FRITTERS EVEN
THOUGH THE DOG WONT EAT THEM WHEN YOU PUT
SALT IN THEM AND

WAIT A SEC

THAT SMOKE ISNT FROM THE TRACTOR ITS
BLOWING ACROSS FROM DOUG THE WRECKER
BURNING OLD TYRES OUT THE BACK OF HIS PLACE

I CANT EVEN SEE THE TRACTOR IN THE SCHOOL
CARPARK ONLY GLOSSOPS CAR AS FLASH AS EVER
AND NOT IN THE RIVER

OH JEEZ RO

THERES THE TRACTOR PARKED IN THE PETROL
STATION WORKSHOP AND THERES YOU SHOWING
THE FUEL TANK TO THE MECHANICS

YOU DROVE IT IN TO GET IT FIXED

YOU KNEW I WAS BUSY IN THE ORCHARD TELLING
THE WEEVILS OFF SO YOU DID IT TO HELP ME OUT

OH LOVE I DUNNO WHAT TO SAY

AS YOUR DAD I SHOULD BE TELLING YOU OFF FOR
RISKING YOUR LIFE BUT INSTEAD IM HAVING A BLUB

I LOVE YOU RO

THERES ONE THING I DONT GET BUT

YOUVE SEEN ME AND YOURE GRINNING AND
WAVING BUT YOURE NOT LOOKING AT YOUR
PHONE JEEZ RO WHY HAVENT YOU ANSWERED MY
MESSAGES AND WHY ARE YOU POINTING AT MY
PHONE

I GET IT YOUVE SENT ME A TEXT MESSAGE OK ILL
READ IT

*G'day Dad. Actions speak louder than words with
texts too. You have to remember to press send.
Love Ro xx :)*

# Give Peas A Chance

'**B**en,' said Mum. 'Eat your veggies.'

Ben didn't hear her. He was too busy staring gloomily at the dead kids on TV.

'Come on, mate,' said Dad. 'A few carrots and zucchini won't kill you. Bung some tomato sauce on them and pretend they're sausages.'

Ben didn't hear him either. This was the third lot of dead kids just on tonight's news.

'Watch out, young man,' said Mum. 'If you don't eat those vegetables now, you might get them cold for breakfast tomorrow. With milk. And only one spoonful of sugar.'

Ben still didn't take his eyes off the TV.

The small blood-stained bodies were lying on a stone floor, arms and legs flopped in different positions like the kids were asleep. Except they weren't asleep, they were dead.

'Ben,' said Dad. 'Did you hear what your

mother just told you?'

Angry men were standing next to the small bodies, yelling and waving guns. Ben could tell they were upset about the dead kids. But this didn't make him feel any better. The men looked like they were yelling for revenge, so by tomorrow night other kids in Iraq would probably have bullets in them too.

'Ben,' said Dad in a voice like a gun going off.

Ben realised the others were all looking at him. Mum wearily, Dad crossly and Claire with that you-are-such-a-der-brain expression big sisters liked so much.

Claire leaned towards him.

'You won't lose any weight skipping veggies,' she said. 'I went on a veggie-free diet last year. Waste of time. You end up eating extra ice-cream to get the vitamins.'

Ben sighed. How could a whole family not see what was happening to the world? Specially now they all had their new contact lenses.

'I don't understand, Ben,' said Mum. 'You like veggies.'

Ben had to admit she was right.

But that was before.

Dad tossed a two-dollar coin onto the table near Ben's plate.

Ben stared at it. Then he realised what Dad was doing. Giving him tomorrow's tuckshop money now. Hoping the thought of tomorrow's jam donut or cream lamington would be enough to help him force down tonight's veggies.

It wasn't.

'Sorry,' said Ben. 'I can't.'

He hadn't planned any of this. It was just sort of happening.

'Why not?' said Dad with that about-to-explode expression dads liked so much.

'Because,' said Ben, 'I'm not eating any more vegetables until people stop shooting each other.'

Later that evening, after Mum and Dad calmed down, Ben explained that his strike wasn't just vegetable-based.

'I won't be tidying my room either,' he said quietly. 'Or clearing the table or taking the bins out or doing homework or being polite to relatives.'

Dad ran his big raw butcher's hands through his thinning hair.

Ben hoped all this wasn't going to make Dad's hair go even more thinning.

For a fleeting moment, Ben was tempted to tell Mum and Dad he was only joking. But he didn't, because he wasn't.

Now I've started this, he thought grimly, I have to keep going.

'This is crazy, Ben,' said Mum. 'People can't change the world even if they want to. Not unless they're Bono or that bloke who invented the iPod. You'll feel different in the morning. Have an early night, there's a good boy.'

'I'm not being a good boy any more,' said Ben. 'Not until grown-ups get rid of all the guns and bombs.'

'Why us?' moaned Dad. 'We haven't got any guns.'

Mum went out to the kitchen and came back. In one hand she had the gas gun for lighting the stove. In the other she had the kitchen waste-bin. She dropped the gas gun into the bin.

'There,' she said to Ben. 'Will you eat your veggies now?'

Ben shook his head.

'Those Iraq and Africa and Palestine people aren't killed by kitchen appliances,' he said.

Mum ran her slim office-manager's hands through her lightly permed hair.

Ben hoped all this wasn't going to make Mum's hair go even more permed.

At bedtime, Claire came into Ben's room for a chat.

'You're making a big mistake, you know,' she said. 'You might think this is a clever way to get out of eating veggies and clearing the table and all that other stuff, but it's not.'

Ben could hear the distant sound of gunfire in the living room. Mum and Dad must be watching the late news.

'I tried something like it last week,' said Claire. 'I told Mum I wasn't going to stop biting my nails unless she let me wear nail polish. So she let me wear some and I forgot and my finger got glued to my mouth.'

Ben looked at his sister's frowning face and, he now saw, her slightly green teeth.

'You must know why I'm doing this,' he said to her. 'You watch the news. Every night there's more and more people being killed in wars. Doesn't it make you upset?'

Claire thought about this.

'Not really,' she said. 'I don't look. Not when I'm eating.'

Ben wished he had that skill.

'When I see those dead people,' he said, 'it makes me think how I'd feel if it was you or Mum or Dad or my friends.'

Claire gave him the der-brain look.

'Don't worry,' she said. 'When the kids at school find out you're behaving like a complete psychiatric, you won't have any friends.'

The kids at school didn't think Ben was behaving like a complete psychiatric.

When he told them he was on strike and wouldn't be eating veggies or clearing the table or tidying his room or taking the bins out or being polite to rellies or doing homework, their part of the playground went quiet and they all looked sort of impressed.

And thoughtful.

'That is such a great excuse, guns and bombs,'

said Skye Borlotti. 'When I want to get out of doing all that stuff, I can only think of things like headaches and pet allergies, and we haven't got any pets.'

'I'm gunna tell my parents they have to get rid of guns and bombs and spiders,' said Shane Moore. 'Our bathroom's a death-trap.'

Several of the other kids started discussing what they were going to add to the list.

Water pistols.

Sticks.

Aunties who kiss.

Ben was a bit worried some of the kids might be missing the point.

He explained about the thousands of people around the world who were killed each day by bullets and explosions, and what it must feel like to have a bullet or a piece of shrapnel go through your head or your mum's head.

The kids all stared at him, even more thoughtful than before.

Shane started to ask how many people were killed by spider bites, then changed his mind.

That night, Ben sat in front of a large plate of steaming vegetables.

He peered at them.

The peas and broccoli looked new, but those carrots and zucchini looked like last night's.

'They are last night's,' said Dad. 'And if you don't eat this lot, they'll be on your plate with tomorrow night's lot.' He shrugged. 'Up to you how long this goes on for.'

Ben frowned as he chewed a mouthful of chop.

He didn't know how long it would go on for, but he was pretty sure the plate probably wouldn't be big enough.

Mum came in from the kitchen, also frowning.

'That was Jean on the phone,' she said. 'Jason's on strike. Veggies, bins, rellies, same nonsense as Ben.'

Dad got his about-to-explode look.

'Typical,' he said. 'There'd have to be one other clown and it'd have to be Jason.'

'Not one,' said Mum. 'Jean's the seventh school parent I've had ringing up complaining tonight.'

Dad stared at her in surprise.

Then Claire gave a yell.

'Look.'

She pointed to the TV. The news had started. On the screen was a headline. Ben had to read it three times to make sure he was seeing it right.

*Kids On Strike.*

'A text-message craze swept the country today,' said the newsreader. 'Thousands of children have gone on the offensive against what one nine-year-old described as weapons that hurt people'.

A girl Ben had never seen before appeared on the screen. She was standing in a milk bar with her arms folded. Behind the counter, looking on proudly, were her parents.

Ben hoped the girl wouldn't say anything about spiders or aunties who kiss.

She didn't.

'I'm not helping in the shop any more,' she said. 'Plus I'm not eating hamburgers, chips, toasted sandwiches or any other hot food or snacks. Not until there's world peace.'

The girl's mother looked even prouder.

Ben felt dazed.

Incredible.

He wanted to hug someone. But he didn't. The available people in the room were all staring at the TV, mouths open.

'Police are investigating,' said the newsreader. 'They say that with the aid of phone records, they will eventually trace the person or persons behind what some commentators are calling un-Australian behaviour.'

Ben had trouble swallowing his mouthful of chop.

Police? Investigating?

Mum, Dad and Claire were all staring at him now with grim faces.

'I tried to warn you,' said Claire.

Ben stayed home the next day.

'I don't want you running around at school causing more trouble,' said Dad as he left for work. 'Keep your head down here till it all blows over.'

'If a SWAT team busts in looking for you,' said

Claire as she grabbed her school bag, 'you can hide in my wardrobe.'

'Don't answer the phone,' said Mum, zipping up her briefcase. 'Your veggies are in the microwave.'

Ben felt too excited to be hungry.

He spent the day on his computer, checking the news sites.

It wasn't blowing over.

Kids all around the country were staying home from school as part of the strike. Others were being driven to school by parents but refusing to get out of the car. Others were sitting in the playground, saying teachers would have to carry them into the classroom. Teachers were refusing because of their backs.

Grown-ups were getting very upset.

Ben felt sorry for them, particularly the vegetable shop owners who were saying they'd go broke if the major world powers didn't seriously rethink their armaments policies.

He knew the same could happen to Dad if kids started not eating meat.

Ben pushed the thought out of his mind. He clicked to another news site.

Incredible.

Kids were going on strike in New Zealand too.

And Japan.

Suddenly Ben felt a bit faint. He wondered if his blood sugar levels were being affected by the speed of the whole thing and how big it was getting.

He went to the kitchen and got a cold sausage from the fridge.

'It'll blow over,' said Dad. 'Just watch.'

Ben looked at the pile of vegetables in front of him. Claire had just done a huge sneeze, but the five nights of veggies heaped on Ben's plate weren't even wobbling.

Ben realised Dad didn't mean the veggies.

'There were crazes when I was a kid,' Dad was saying. 'Pointy shoes. Disco. Smurfs. Hoola hoops. Mohawk hairdos. They all blew over.'

Mum gave Dad a look. She pointed to the TV screen, where a classroom full of Tibetan students were sitting at their desks, ignoring the bowls of yak's-milk porridge going cold in front of them.

'Didn't you hear what the news just said?' demanded Mum. 'Two hundred and thirty million kids in eighty-six countries have gone on strike. I don't think mohawk hairdos were ever quite that popular.'

Dad stared at the screen too.

His shoulders sagged.

He turned to Ben, not looking cross any more, just very worried.

'Why couldn't you have eaten your veggies?' he said pleadingly.

Ben didn't know what to say. He was feeling a bit stunned. He also hated seeing Mum and Dad unhappy, but that was partly why he was doing this, so it would be a safer happier world for them to grow old in.

The front door bell rang.

Claire went to answer it.

She came back looking frightened.

'It's the federal police,' she said.

After posing for photos with Ben on the steps of Parliament House, the Minister for Defence spoke briefly to the crowd of reporters.

'I salute the vision of this young Australian,' he said. 'The government shares his desire for a peaceful world. But unfortunately guns and missiles and our new fighter-bombers with their laser-tracking capability are a necessary evil. To have peace we must be well-armed.'

Ben took a deep breath and spoke up.

'Excuse me, your honour,' he said. 'But if nobody else was armed, why would we need to be?'

The defence minister smiled for quite a long time.

'Young people get confused,' he said to the cameras. 'It's up to you, parents of Australia. Explain it to them.'

Ben saw that Mum was looking a bit doubtful.

'Could you just run through the main points?' she said to the defence minister.

The minister hesitated, then smiled some more.

'I know it's not easy,' he said to the cameras. 'I'm a parent too.'

Dad was looking thoughtful.

He nodded towards Ben.

'If you were his father,' Dad said to the minister, 'how would you get him to eat his veggies?'

For a horrible moment Ben thought the minister was going to announce a new law with on-the-spot fines for kids who wouldn't eat all their dinner.

Instead, Claire spoke up.

'Do you think any countries'll get rid of their guns?' she asked the defence minister loudly so the reporters could hear.

The defence minister stopped grinning and shook his head.

'Not a chance,' he said.

The first country to get rid of its guns was Iceland.

Ben stared at the TV, struggling to stay calm, a piece of roast pork unchewed in his mouth.

Mum and Dad and Claire stopped chewing too.

'Unreal,' said Claire.

'We're doing it for our children,' said the Icelandic prime minister, standing next to a big drilling machine that was drilling into the ice. 'We've decided to bury our weapons in this glacier, so future generations of young Icelanders will be able to see them in the ice and think about how much better off we are without them.'

'And are you also doing it,' said one of a large group of journalists, 'so the current generation of young Icelanders will get out of bed and start eating fish again?'

'Yes,' said the Icelandic prime minister. 'That as well.'

Ben realised the rest of the family had stopped looking at the TV and were all looking at him.

So were the reporters outside the lounge room window.

Dad reached over and squeezed Ben's shoulder.

'Incredible,' he said in a stunned voice.

'Well done, love,' said Mum to Ben, sounding pretty stunned herself. 'Now will you eat your veggies?'

'Not yet,' said Ben.

Other countries tried to keep their guns.

'Hey,' yelled a reporter to Ben. 'Egypt has banned all pictures of shot and blown-up people on their TV. Any comment?'

Ben knew he wasn't meant to answer journalists who yelled at him through the lounge room window. But Mum was in the bathroom and he couldn't resist.

'If I was an Egyptian kid,' he yelled back, 'I'd draw a picture in coloured crayons of what happens when a toddler gets hit by a machine gun bullet and I'd stick the picture on my parents' TV screen.'

Two days later, the same journalist was yelling at Ben again.

'Two million Egyptian kids followed your suggestion,' he shouted. 'Any comment?'

'See what you've done now, Ben,' said Mum in

an exasperated voice as she pulled the curtains. 'I told you not to talk to the media.'

The next country to get rid of its guns was Taiwan.

'Good on you, Taiwan,' said Dad as he turned up the sound on the TV.

Mum glanced at Ben's plate.

Ben pretended not to notice.

'We're doing it for our economy,' said the Taiwanese president, standing next to a brand new recycling plant for ferrous and non-ferrous metals. 'Melting down these guns will allow us to make many more MP3 players.'

'And are you also doing it,' said a journalist, 'so the young people of Taiwan will get out of bed and start buying MP3 players again?'

'Yes,' said the Taiwanese president. 'That as well.'

Ben helped Dad find Taiwan in the atlas.

'It's next to China,' said Mum.

Dad put a big tick with a marker pen on the map of Taiwan.

'Two down,' said Dad, studying the list of countries in the front of the atlas. 'A hundred and twenty-three to go.'

'I wish they'd hurry up,' said Mum, staring wearily at the huge pile of uneaten veggies on Ben's plate.

When China saw that Taiwan didn't have any guns, they decided to invade.

Millions of Chinese children lay down in front of the war planes and tanks. The Chinese authorities arrested the parents of every child involved. And the aunties, and the uncles, and the people who weren't really relatives but helped out with child-minding after school.

'Any comment?' yelled the reporters in Ben's front yard.

Ben didn't have any comment.

Not to the reporters.

Silently he worried that things might be getting a bit out of control, and that it was all his fault.

'I'll send an email to the Chinese embassy,' said Claire. 'Remind them they've got the Olympics coming up.'

Soon the Chinese authorities started releasing people from jail.

Chinese children stayed on strike.

China started getting rid of its weapons.

'They had to,' said Claire to Ben. 'Most of their athletes are under eighteen. Plus who'll vacuum the Olympic stadiums if all the adults are in jail?'

'Thanks, Claire,' said Ben. 'I'm glad you're on our side.'

When the other countries saw China had got rid of its weapons, they did too.

America was last.

They made excuses and broke promises and pretended they didn't have enough recycling depots.

'That's bull,' said Mum indignantly. 'They can turn all their gun shops and missile silos into recycling depots.'

Ben grinned. Trust an office manager to get things organised.

Finally the US Congress persuaded the president to sign the disarmament bill by explaining the terrible damage that would be done to the US economy if American kids continued not to eat McDonald's.

'Come on, Ben,' said Mum. 'You've got no excuses now. Eat your veggies.'

Ben knew it was Mum from her voice. He couldn't actually see her because of the mountain of vegetables on the serving platter in front of him.

She sounded tired.

Ben wasn't surprised.

They were all tired after weeks of living in the media spotlight. Thank goodness the footy season had started and a couple of coaches had been sacked and the media had all gone to their front yards.

'Look,' said Claire, pointing to the TV screen.

Ben peered around his veggies.

On the TV news, the last gun from the last warship in the world was being melted down in San Diego.

'You heard your mother, Ben,' said Dad. 'You've got your own way, you've brought peace to the entire planet, now you have to keep your side of the bargain. Eat those veggies.'

Ben looked at Dad's proud grin and the relieved expression on Mum's face.

World peace felt good.

He stuck his fork into a big lump of much-microwaved broccoli, put it into his mouth and started chewing.

All next day at school, even while people were saying how nice it was to have him back, Ben couldn't stop thinking about how long it was going to take him to eat that pile of veggies.

About a year, probably.

Longer if he kept getting sick of their fridge-taste as quickly as he had last night.

But later, when Ben sat down at the dinner table, he stared in surprise.

The mountain of veggies had been divided into four smaller piles. Mum, Dad and Claire each had a pile on their plate. They were eating the veggies as fast as they could.

'Thanks,' said Ben.

What a generous family.

'We're not doing it for you,' said Claire through a mouthful of spinach.

She pointed to the TV screen.

Ben stared. The news report was describing how two hours ago America had invaded Iran. On the screen, American warplanes and bombers hurtled over Tehran.

'But they haven't got any guns or bombs,' said

Ben. 'How can they declare war?'

'Veggies,' said Dad grimly.

At first Ben didn't understand. Then he saw what the bombers were dropping from high altitude onto the panicked Iranian people.

Cauliflower.

Pumpkin.

Mashed potato with really big lumps in it.

'That is disgusting,' said Mum. 'Targeting kids like that.'

On the TV a fighter plane roared low over a block of flats. Every window exploded into shards of glass under a hail of frozen brussel sprouts and sweetcorn.

Ben stared in horror.

'Don't just sit there gawking,' said Claire. 'Eat your veggies.'

'The more we can eat,' said Mum through a mouthful of carrot, 'the less there'll be to injure innocent civilians.'

Ben nodded.

He looked at his family, all doing their bit to make the world a better place.

Then he stuffed a big forkful of peas into his mouth and chewed as fast as he could.

# Good Dog

**V**eronica looks horrified when I arrive at her party.

She stands at the front door, her mouth open. The fluffy balls on her party dress wobble with alarm. The fake jewels on her tiara tremble with panic.

'Happy birthday,' I say.

She's not even looking at me, she's staring at Anthony.

'Woof,' says Anthony.

'A dog?' squeaks Veronica. 'Ginger, why did you bring a dog? My dad's not good with dogs.'

'I couldn't afford a present,' I explain. 'So I brought Anthony. You've been saying all week you hope your party will be a success. Well, Anthony's here to help. He's a party dog.'

Veronica gives a little whimper.

'Don't worry,' I say. 'I know Anthony's big, but he's friendly. He won't hurt your dog.'

Veronica glances nervously over my shoulder.

'Our dog isn't here,' she says. 'My dad's in the park, training it.'

She doesn't have to tell me. I can hear Mr Pobjoy's angry voice drifting over from the park across the road.

'Bad dog,' he's yelling. 'Bad dog.'

I swap a look with Anthony.

Mr Pobjoy should be in the army. We live two streets away and most evenings I can hear him roaring at that poor dog even over the noise of Mum and Dad's music in the kitchen.

Anthony hates hearing another dog being treated like that. Usually he sticks his head under one of our cats so he doesn't have to listen to it.

Now he just wants to get inside.

'Stop,' says Veronica to Anthony. 'Come back.'

Anthony has squeezed past her into the house.

'Party dogs hate having to wait outside,' I explain. 'They want to get in and start partying.'

We hurry inside after Anthony.

The party is in the family room. About ten kids are on leather chairs in front of a huge TV. The boys are fighting and the girls are complaining and they're all throwing party food at each other.

'Good grief,' says Veronica's mum when she sees Anthony. 'That's all I need.'

Mrs Pobjoy is very stressed. Her fashionable clothes have got quite a lot of marshmallow dip on them. Her very fashionable hair, which Mum reckons would cost more to have done than some countries spend on food, is looking a bit sweat-affected.

'Is that your dog?' Mrs Pobjoy says to me.

'Yes,' I say. 'His name's Anthony. I'm Ginger. I sit next to Veronica in class.'

I hold out my hand to shake Mrs Pobjoy's. She doesn't see it.

'Pets were not invited,' she says to Veronica.

'I didn't invite it,' says Veronica miserably. 'She just arrived with it.'

'It's OK,' I say to Mrs Pobjoy. 'Anthony's here to help.'

Mrs Pobjoy still looks stressed.

I explain to her how Anthony was already a party expert when I got him. How when I first saw him in the pound he was playing What's The Time Mr Wolf with all the other dogs. Letting them creep up behind him, then turning and chasing them till they nearly wet themselves with excitement.

'That is the stupidest thing I've ever heard,' says Mrs Pobjoy crossly.

'It's not,' I say. 'Anthony's a mixture of wolfhound and English sheepdog. Wolfhounds are very fun-loving and English sheepdogs have to organise a lot of party games out in the fields to keep the sheep warm in winter.'

'Get it out of here,' says Mrs Pobjoy.

'Look,' says Veronica, pointing.

Anthony is already rounding up the kids for

121

the first game, nudging and nuzzling them off the couch. When someone doesn't want to move, Anthony grabs a corner of their party frock or best shirt between his teeth and gently drags them.

Some of the kids are screaming and trying to run away. Others are trying to hide under the chairs. This always happens when Anthony arrives at a party. Kids get over-excited.

'The first game's Hide And Seek,' I say to the screamers and runners. 'It's fun. Do what the others are doing. Hide somewhere you don't think Anthony will find you.'

Kids hurl themselves into cupboards and clamber up onto shelves.

Soon everyone is hidden. Except for Mrs Pobjoy, who is outside in the barbeque area, glowering at Anthony and talking very fast into her mobile.

Anthony starts finding everyone.

Some people are so worked up they almost faint when Anthony sticks his big head into the laundry basket or nest of tables they're hiding in. He does have very big teeth, which can be a bit of a problem for a party organiser.

But when he licks your face, which is his way of saying *good hiding place, but I found you*, you know he wouldn't hurt a fly. Not even an over-excited fly who's had way too many lollies.

By the end of the game, some kids are grinning. Even Veronica isn't looking so upset, probably because she won by hiding in her dad's wine cellar.

'Good on you,' I whisper to Anthony.

He made sure he found Veronica last. That's the advantage of being a mixture of breeds. You get to be not only clever, but also kind on birthdays.

'What's next?' someone yells.

Anthony is already organising the next game, wagging his big tail and herding everybody into a line.

'Musical Chairs,' I say, grabbing the dining chairs and putting them into a line too.

Anthony starts singing. Well, howling really. He can sort of do some of Mum and Dad's Rod Stewart tunes. Well, bits of them.

A few of the kids look like they want to go back to playing Hide And Seek.

I know why. When Anthony sings, he does spray quite a lot of saliva around. It's the one other problem he has as a party organiser.

But his timing's great. He waits for me to whisk another chair away, then stops howling at really unexpected moments. Each time he does, kids are laughing and falling over each other to get their bums on a seat.

Veronica is laughing too. She can see her party's going really well.

Then a loud voice booms out.

'Whoa. What's going on here?'

The room goes quiet. We all turn and see a man in a business suit standing in the doorway. He's got a mobile phone in one hand and a very small white dog in the other.

'It's OK, Dad,' pleads Veronica. 'We're having a really good time. Anthony's a really good party org . . .'

Her voice trails off. Mr Pobjoy is glaring at her.

'Bad girl,' he says.

Veronica tries to shrink inside her party dress.

Mr Pobjoy points at Anthony.

'What are you thinking, Veronica,' he says, 'bringing a brute like that in here? It could tear Flossy Evangeline Diamante to pieces. Good grief, you know how much we paid for Flossy.'

Veronica is close to tears.

'Two thousand dollars,' she says in a tiny voice.

The rest of us stare at the little white dog in amazement. That must work out at more than a thousand dollars a kilo. Even Anthony is looking stunned.

'Poor little Flossy,' says Mr Pobjoy. 'Look at her. She's trembling. She's terrified.'

No she's not. She's curled up contentedly and looking down at Anthony with keen interest. Veronica's the one who's trembling and upset.

Suddenly Flossy jumps down from Mr Pobjoy's hand, trots over to Anthony and starts sniffing his bottom. Well, sniffing his legs, because there's no way she can reach his bottom without a small ladder.

'Flossy,' snaps Mr Pobjoy. 'Come back here.'

Flossy ignores him.

'Bad dog,' he yells at her. 'Bad dog.'

Flossy still ignores him.

Anthony gives her a sniff because that's the polite thing to do. And also, I can tell, because he feels a bit protective. She's a small dog being yelled at by a big man.

'Bad dog,' roars Mr Pobjoy again.

Anthony tilts his head down next to Flossy's and gently licks her ear a few times. It's almost like he's whispering to her.

Suddenly Flossy trots back over to Mr Pobjoy, who gives an angry but satisfied nod.

Flossy stops right next to his feet and pees on his shoes.

'Bad dog,' yells Mr Pobjoy, jumping back and trying to shake the pee off his feet, his voice going squeaky with outrage.

The rest of us are trying not to laugh. Several of the kids aren't managing it very well. I see Anthony looking at me with his big brown eyes and something in his expression gives me an idea. I speak up before Veronica's dad sends us all home.

'Mr Pobjoy,' I say. 'I'm quite experienced with dogs and I know how hard it can be to train them. One thing that's worked really well for me is a party game called Good Dog Bad Dog.'

Mr Pobjoy looks at me long and hard.

I can see that what he really wants to do is chuck us all out so he can yell at Flossy and Veronica in private. But he's been trying to train Flossy for weeks. Underneath his expensive suit and his hair transplant, I'm guessing he's desperate.

'Please, Dad,' says Veronica. 'Give it a go.'

'Good Dog Bad Dog?' mutters Mr Pobjoy, not sounding convinced.

Mrs Pobjoy has been off and changed her clothes and she's looking a bit less stressed.

'You might as well give it a go, Vince,' she says wearily to her husband. 'You've said yourself Flossy is a difficult dog.'

Mr Pobjoy frowns suspiciously.

'How does this game work?' he says.

'It's simple,' I say. 'For the next five minutes, all we're allowed to say is either *good dog* or *bad dog*.'

Mr Pobjoy looks doubtful.

Please, I urge him silently. Give it a go.

My plan is dead simple. To show Mr Pobjoy that kindness gets better results than yelling. Though you'd think a top business manager like him would already know that.

'OK,' I say. 'Let's start.'

I look at Anthony to make sure he understands what we're doing. I can tell from the way he looks at me that he does.

I'm going to say *good dog* to him lots of times and he's going to do lots of clever tricks and obedient things to show Mr Pobjoy that *good dog* always works better than *bad dog*.

Flossy is sniffing Anthony's leg again. Anthony

126

starts licking Flossy's ear again in a murmuring sort of way.

Before I can get my first *good dog* out, Mr Pobjoy, whose shoes are still wet, turns to Anthony.

'Bad dog,' he snaps.

Anthony looks at him for a moment, then does something that isn't really what you'd expect from a good dog.

He leans forward, opens his huge jaws, places them around Flossy, and closes them.

Flossy disappears.

Inside Anthony's mouth.

Veronica screams.

So do the other kids.

Mrs Pobjoy clutches the pool table.

I feel faint. I can hear the distant echo of something a dog-hater once said to me. That you can never trust pound dogs. That sooner or later they always turn vicious.

Then I see Anthony is looking at me. He isn't chewing or swallowing, just looking at me patiently. The bulge in his mouth is still moving.

Suddenly I know what he's doing.

He isn't turning vicious, he's just playing Good Dog Bad Dog his way.

'No,' howls Mr Pobjoy. 'Flossy. That brute has eaten Flossy.'

I turn to Veronica, whose fluffy party-dress balls are trembling almost as much as her lips.

'Rescue Flossy,' I whisper to Veronica. 'You won't

get hurt, I promise. Just say *good dog*.'

Veronica stares at me.

I can see this isn't the birthday party she was hoping for.

'Better hurry,' I whisper. 'Flossy's running out of air in there.'

Veronica goes nervously over to Anthony. She has to step around her father, who is yelling insulting things at Anthony again.

'Bad dog,' he's shouting. 'Bad dog. Bad dog.'

Anthony ignores him and turns to face Veronica, his jaws still closed.

I can just make out faint tremors of movement inside his mouth.

Veronica hesitates. Then I see Anthony looking into her eyes and I know everything's going to be OK.

Veronica can hardly get the words out.

But she does.

'Good dog,' she whispers to Anthony.

'Mr Pobjoy,' I say. 'Look. Veronica's saving Flossy.'
And she is.

'Good dog,' she says, and Anthony slowly opens his mouth. Veronica puts her hands inside and lifts out a soggy, bedraggled, stunned-looking Flossy.

'Woof,' says Flossy.

'Good dog,' says Veronica.

'Thank God,' says Mr Pobjoy, taking Flossy from Veronica. 'Flossy, sweetie. It's OK, you're safe. Good dog. Good dog.'

He hugs Flossy.

'Good dog,' he says, over and over.

Then he hugs Veronica.

'Good girl,' he says to her. 'Good girl.'

Veronica is tearful again, but in a way that lets us all see this is the best party she's ever had.

'Good on you,' I whisper to Anthony.

Mr Pobjoy stops hugging Flossy and Veronica, and looks over at me and Anthony.

'I think it's best,' he says tersely, 'if you both leave.'

Then he goes back to hugging his dog and his daughter.

I don't argue.

On the way out, Veronica's mum catches up with us.

'Thank you,' she says. 'Thank you both so much. Veronica's cousin is having a party next week. I don't suppose you and Anthony can come?'

'That's very kind,' I say. 'I think we can.'

I check with Anthony.

He licks my hand.

I can see he likes the idea of another party.

We both do.

# Cornflakes

That morning I didn't have the faintest inkling my life was about to change forever. So I just did what a ten-year-old boy normally does first thing. Padded sleepily to the toilet and had a pee.

I watched it spurt out.

Why, I wondered, does the first pee of the day always look like chicken soup?

I hadn't had any chicken soup for weeks. So if it was chicken soup, why had it taken so long to reach my willy? And why would chicken soup only drain out first thing in the morning?

Gradually, as the pee trickled out of me, so did my sleepiness.

My thoughts got clearer.

I realised it probably wasn't chicken soup. It didn't smell like chicken soup, and there were no vegetables in it.

*

Now, all these years later, I know the truth.

My pee wasn't chicken soup, it was much more interesting than that.

Like all human urine it was a deadly aqueous solution of salts, minerals, vitamins, corpuscles, uric acid, nitrogenous waste products, organic compounds, and chemicals from lollies.

When it splashed into the toilet bowl, there was widespread carnage. Most of the hundreds of millions of tiny organisms who had spent the night floating in the toilet water without a care in the world were killed instantly.

Peed to death.

Please don't blame me.

I didn't know then.

My family didn't know either.

My mother didn't have a clue, as she cleaned her shoes over the kitchen sink, that she was wiping out a microbe population bigger than the human population of Australia, including Tasmania.

My big sister Sarah had no idea, as she delicately removed a wax-based community from one of her ears with a fingernail and ate it, that she was a mass-murderer of mind-boggling proportions.

My father didn't suspect, as he waited for the toaster to finish its work, that he was searing and scorching countless tiny bread creatures and turning them into, well, toast.

The only member of the family who did suspect

something was my little sister Nell.

'Nell,' said Mother. 'Eat your cornflakes, love.'

Mother pointed to me.

'Look,' she said, 'Timmy's eating his.'

Nell pushed the bowl away.

In those days, I thought Nell was just a cute little kid who didn't know much.

I was wrong.

Nell already suspected that if she ate her cornflakes, innocent creatures would die. But it wasn't the millions of cowering proteobacteria trying not to draw attention to themselves on the surface of the milk in her bowl that she had in mind.

'Nell,' said Mother. 'Why don't you want to eat your cornflakes?'

'Because of the fairies,' said Nell.

Mother and Father looked at each other and tried not to smile.

One thing I did know was that adults could sometimes be a bit hurtful, even when they were loving parents who didn't mean to be, and that sometimes little sisters needed a brother on their side.

'Fairies?' I said to Nell. 'Where?'

'In the cornflakes,' said Nell. She pointed to a picture of a fairy on the cornflakes box. 'See?'

Now Mother and Father did smile.

'You're so funny,' said Sarah, giving Nell a tickle. 'And dopey.'

I've never approved of younger sisters being

called dopey, so I gave Sarah a look. And I gave Mother and Father one too, just in case they were thinking of using the same word.

'Nell,' I said gently. 'We've taken the fairy out, remember?'

I pointed to the plastic fairy standing next to Nell's dish, plastic wand raised, plastic wings bejewelled with cornflake dust.

'Not that fairy,' said Nell, getting annoyed. 'The other fairies. The tiny ones. In the cornflakes.'

Sarah struggled not to laugh. She put her hand over her mouth and millions of finger microbes found themselves having a travel experience they hadn't expected.

I spoke up quickly before somebody said something else that hurt Nell's feelings.

'There's only one fairy,' I explained gently to her, pointing to the side of the cornflakes box. 'It says so here.'

Because Nell couldn't read yet, I did it for her.

'*One fairy per carton.*'

Nell didn't look convinced.

'Come on, sweetie,' said Father. 'Eat up.'

Nell shook her head.

'The box is wrong,' she said.

'Those cornflakes manufacturers are mean,' I said to Nell. 'Only putting one fairy in each box.'

'Tell you what,' said Mother to Nell. 'How about Timmy has the first spoonful of your cornflakes to prove there are no more fairies?'

I wasn't sure about this. I felt like we were all ganging up on Nell. But Mother and Father were both looking at me pleadingly.

I scooped some of Nell's cornflakes and milk onto my spoon and lifted it to my mouth.

Nell's pudgy little jaw started to quiver and behind her blonde curls her dark eyes filled with tears.

I hesitated.

I wanted to help, not hurt.

'If you scare fairies by trying to eat them,' said Nell fiercely, 'they make you sneeze.'

I looked at Mother and Father to see what I should do.

Father gave a little nod of encouragement.

I put the cornflakes into my mouth and chewed.

Up my nose, chaos broke out. Several million nasal-passage microbes, alarmed by the sudden proximity of the proteobacteria in the milk, tried to crowd into my sinuses.

My mucus membranes got seriously trampled, my cilia became inflamed, the whole subcutaneous region went tickly, and I sneezed a spray of cornflakes and milk across the table.

Nobody moved. Except Nell, who picked a bit of soggy cornflake off her face and put it back into her bowl.

'See?' she said.

Nobody else said anything for a moment.

I stared at the bowl of cornflakes, and in that instant I felt my whole life change.

Then Father spoke.

'It's OK, sweetie,' he said to Nell. 'You don't have to eat your cornflakes if you don't want to.'

'Oh dear, Timmy,' said Mother. 'I think you might be coming down with something. I'm going to make you some chicken soup.'

I didn't reply.

I was too busy staring at the cornflakes and wondering if I had enough money in my junior saver account to buy a microscope.

Many years later, when I was a professor at university, I told a class of students about Nell and how she'd changed my life.

I brought my first microscope along to show them, and as I took it out of its battered old box, I knew exactly what they were going to ask. So I gave them the answer before anyone even spoke.

'Not powerful enough,' I said, shaking my head and giving my dear old junior microscope a fond polish.

I don't teach at the university any more. I went on to become a research scientist, and I've been one for over thirty years now.

Last year one of my ex-students came to visit. He was very kind and congratulated me on being what he called one of the most brilliant research scientists in the world.

'I'm not really,' I replied. 'Not compared to my little sister Nell. She's the one who is truly brilliant.'

I could see the ex-student thought I was just being modest. He'd forgotten what I'd told him that day in class about how I owe my whole career to Nell.

He's remembered now.

A few months ago Nell won the Nobel prize for her work developing the most powerful microscope ever. The one that uses fixed orbiting satellites to increase its focal length.

That ex-student was one of thousands of people who sent Nell messages congratulating her on the prize.

She deserves it.

It isn't easy being the youngest. You get a bit overshadowed. Specially when everyone thinks your older brother is the brilliant one, plus your older sister owns the biggest pest-exterminating business in the world.

It hasn't been easy for Nell as a scientist, either.

When you're doing research that's a bit different, other scientists can sometimes be hurtful even when they don't mean to be, and sometimes little sisters need a brother on their side.

I was with Nell in the lab yesterday when she finally did the thing our colleagues said could never be done.

She turned from her microscope, eyes shining with excitement.

'Look,' she said.

I looked into the microscope, the one Nell had invented. I looked for a long time.

'I knew you'd do it,' I said.

Scientists aren't meant to get emotional, but we both laughed and shouted and danced. Which can sometimes happen when scientists have a breakthrough in the research project they've been working on for years.

Then we went to our favourite restaurant and celebrated with chicken soup.

I can't go into too much detail about our breakthrough because the official announcement hasn't been made yet, but I can say it's a remarkable discovery involving cornflakes.

# My First Ever Go At Bomb Disposal

## A Play by Ned Timms

**NOTE** – *If you do this play at home or in class, please make sure the part of Mum is performed by somebody under 35 as she's getting a bit sensitive about her age.*

**SCENE ONE**
ME AND MUM SITTING IN A TRAIN AT CENTRAL STATION WAITING TO GO TO AUNTY KATH'S IN LEURA FOR AFTERNOON TEA AND HUNDREDS OF HOURS OF GROWN-UP TALK. THE TRAIN ISN'T LEAVING FOR ANOTHER SIX MINUTES AND I'M BORED ALREADY.

**ME**    I'm bored already.

**MUM**   Don't start love. Read your book.

**ME**    I forgot it.

**MUM**     Well listen to your MP3.

**ME**     I forgot that too.

**MUM**     I left it on the kitchen table for you. How could you forget it?

**ME**     I must have put my book on it.

MUM DOES ONE OF THOSE LOOKS SHE DOES WHEN SHE FORGETS THAT PEOPLE ARE ONLY HUMAN.

**MUM**     Right young man well you're not sitting here for a two-hour train trip whingeing the whole way so you'll have to think of something else to do. You didn't forget your imagination did you?

**ME**     No Mum.

**MUM**     Well use it.

**ME**     How do you mean?

**MUM**     I don't know Ned it's your imagination.

MUM STARTS READING HER BOOK WHICH IS ALL RIGHT FOR HER, SHE HASN'T INHERITED DAD'S BAD MEMORY.

**ME**      I spy with my little eye something beginning
          with X.

MUM DOESN'T ANSWER. SHE HATES I-SPY.

**ME**      Xpress train.

A MAN GETS ON THE TRAIN AND SITS A FEW
SEATS AWAY FROM US. HE HAS QUITE DARK
SKIN AND A BLACK MOUSTACHE AND A BRIEFCASE
AND FOREIGN CLOTHES. I LOOK AT HIM FOR
A WHILE. SOME OF THE OTHER PASSENGERS
LOOK AT HIM TOO. SUDDENLY I HAVE A SCARY
THOUGHT.

**ME**      (WHISPERING) Mum.

**MUM**    Mmmm?

**ME**      What if that man's a terrorist?

**MUM**    Eh? What man?

**ME**      (POINTING) That man sitting over there.

**MUM**    Don't be silly. And don't point.

**ME**      He could be. He's foreign and he looks like
          the terrorists on telly and he's wearing a

terrorist kaftan thing like you used to wear
when you didn't want people to see you
were fat.

**MUM**    Ned. Enough.

**ME**    Maybe we should tell somebody.

**MUM**    Be quiet.

MUM HAS GOT HER TEETH CLENCHED LIKE SHE'S
STRUGGLING NOT TO PANIC. SHE GIVES THE MAN
AND THE OTHER PASSENGERS A FAKE SMILE.

**MUM**    I'm sorry, please excuse my son.

THE MAN SMILES BACK. IF HE'S A TERRORIST HE
MUST BE REALLY WELL-TRAINED BECAUSE YOU
CAN'T TELL IF HIS SMILE IS FAKE OR REAL.

**MAN**    Is OK. Is happy time to travel with children.

**MUM**    Mmmm.

THE MAN STOPS SMILING. SUDDENLY HE LOOKS
VERY SAD LIKE HE'S THINKING OF BAD THINGS
HE'S DONE IN THE PAST FOR EXAMPLE BLOWING UP
BUILDINGS, OR ELSE BAD THINGS HE'S PLANNING
TO DO IN THE FUTURE FOR EXAMPLE BLOWING UP
THIS TRAIN.

**MUM**    Say sorry Ned.

**ME**    Sorry.

**MUM**    Not to me, to the gentleman.

BEFORE I CAN, THE MAN JUMPS UP.

**MAN**    Please to protect my seat.

THE MAN GETS OFF THE TRAIN.

**MUM**    I despair of you sometimes Ned. You've hurt his feelings and the train's leaving in four minutes.

I STARE AT THE MAN'S EMPTY SEAT WHICH ISN'T AS EMPTY AS I'D LIKE IT TO BE.

**ME**    Mum, look.

I POINT. MY FINGER IS TREMBLING. SOMETIMES WHEN YOU STRUGGLE TO STAY CALM ALL THE PANIC GOES TO YOUR FINGER.

**MUM**    An innocent businessman, and just because he comes from Iran or Iraq or somewhere . . .

**ME**    He's left his briefcase.

THE MAN'S BRIEFCASE IS SITTING ON HIS SEAT.
MUM STOPS YAKKING. SHE STARES AT THE
BRIEFCASE JUST LIKE I'M DOING AND SEVERAL
OF THE OTHER PASSENGERS ARE DOING TOO.

**ME**     What if it's a bomb?

A COUPLE OF THE OTHER PASSENGERS MOVE TO
OTHER SEATS.

**MUM**    Don't be silly.

**ME**     It could be, you don't know.

**MUM**    Ned I'm losing patience.

**ME**     Ring the army bomb disposal squad. Or
the police if you haven't got the army bomb
disposal squad's number.

**MUM**    Ned . . .

**ME**     On the platform it said we should report all
unattended luggage. (POINTS) That luggage
is totally unattended.

**MUM**    Ned, sit down and stop pointing.

SOMETIMES MUM GETS A TONE IN HER VOICE
THAT IS VERY SCARY. NOT AS SCARY AS A BOMB

ON A TRAIN, BUT SCARY. I SIT BACK DOWN. OTHER
PASSENGERS SIT BACK DOWN AS WELL.

**MUM**    There's probably a simple explanation.

**ME**    Like what? The train leaves in two minutes.
Name one possible thing.

**MUM**    I don't know, he could be getting a paper.

I THINK ABOUT THIS.

**ME**    He's foreign. He probably can't read English.

MUM THINKS ABOUT THIS.

**MUM**    He could be getting a snack.

I THINK ABOUT THIS.

**ME**    What if he's only allowed to eat special
foreign food? The station only sells
Australian pies and Australian sandwiches
and Australian lollies and Australian chewing
gum.

MUM THINKS ABOUT THIS.

**MUM**    He could be ringing his family from a public
phone because he hasn't got a mobile.

I THINK ABOUT THIS.

**ME**     He's got a briefcase. People who have
           briefcases always have mobiles.

MUM DOES ONE OF THOSE LOOKS SHE DOES WHEN
SHE FORGETS THAT SOMETIMES OTHER PEOPLE
ARE RIGHT EVEN WHEN THEY'RE YOUNGER THAN
HER.

**MUM**    For goodness sake Ned use your imagination
           he could be going to the toilet or getting
           some exercise or having a quick coffee or
           asking for a timetable or picking up some
           dry-cleaning or sniffing the flowers on the
           flower stall or looking for an umbrella he left
           in the ticket office or buying an MP3 player.

MUM SLUMPS BACK IN HER SEAT, OUT OF BREATH.

**ME**     If you're right, why didn't he take his
           briefcase?

MUM DOESN'T HAVE AN ANSWER TO THAT. I LOOK
AT HER IN TRIUMPH. I'VE WON. THEN I REMEMBER
I HAVEN'T WON. WE'RE ON A TRAIN WITH A BOMB.
THE TRAIN GIVES A JOLT AND STARTS MOVING.

**ME**     Quick Mum, open the window.

I FLING MYSELF AT THE BRIEFCASE. SOME OF
THE OTHER PASSENGERS SCREAM. I SNATCH THE
BRIEFCASE OFF THE SEAT. AS I SWING IT TOWARDS
THE WINDOW THE CATCH BREAKS BECAUSE OF A
MANUFACTURING FAULT AND EVERYTHING TUMBLES
OUT ONTO THE FLOOR. BOOKS, TEA BAGS, PENS,
TISSUES, PHOTOS, FRUIT, BITS OF PAPER, COUGH
LOLLIES.

NO BOMB.

I STARE AT THE STUFF ON THE FLOOR TO MAKE
DOUBLE SURE THERE ISN'T A BOMB. THEN I
START GRABBING THE THINGS AND PUTTING
THEM BACK INTO THE BRIEFCASE. I PICK UP
A PHOTO. THE MAN'S IN IT AND A WOMAN
AND A GIRL AND A BOY ALL IN FOREIGN CLOTHES.
THEN I PICK UP A PIECE OF OLD NEWSPAPER
WRAPPED IN CLEAR PLASTIC. I READ THE
HEADLINE – *REFUGEE BOAT SINKS, 353 DROWN,
MOSTLY WOMEN AND CHILDREN.*

**MAN**   Please, let me.

I LOOK UP. THE MAN IS BACK. HE'S STANDING
THERE HOLDING THREE ICE-CREAMS CAREFULLY
IN A BUNCH LIKE THEY'RE REALLY PRECIOUS.

**MAN**   One you, one your mother.

147

FOR A MOMENT I'M NOT SURE WHAT TO DO. I STAND
UP. I TAKE TWO OF THE ICE-CREAMS.

**ME**    Um, thank you.

I SIT DOWN NEXT TO MUM AND GIVE HER AN ICE-
CREAM. SHE GIVES IT BACK TO ME AND STANDS UP
AND GOES OVER TO THE MAN.

**MUM**    That's very kind. You shouldn't have.
Thank you.

MUM HELPS THE MAN PUT THE THINGS BACK INTO
HIS BRIEFCASE. SHE SEES THE PHOTO AND THE
PIECE OF NEWSPAPER. I CAN SEE SHE WANTS TO
SAY SOMETHING TO THE MAN BUT SHE CAN'T THINK
OF ANYTHING. SHE TOUCHES HIS ARM. HE LOWERS
HIS EYES.

MUM SITS BACK DOWN. SO DOES THE MAN. I GIVE
MUM HER ICE-CREAM.

THE TRAIN'S GOING FAST NOW. I EAT MY ICE-CREAM.
I THINK ABOUT THE THINGS IN THE MAN'S
BRIEFCASE. SPECIALLY THE PICTURES OF HIS FAMILY.

I FEEL SAD.

I LOOK AT MUM. SHE LOOKS SAD TOO. SHE'S NOT
EATING HER ICE-CREAM.

**MUM**   You have it love.

I EAT HER ICE-CREAM.

WHEN I'VE FINISHED I LOOK OVER AT THE MAN.
HE'S NOT EATING HIS ICE-CREAM EITHER. IT'S
MELTING. LITTLE TRICKLES ARE RUNNING ONTO HIS
HAND. HE DOESN'T NOTICE BECAUSE HIS EYES ARE
CLOSED. LITTLE TRICKLES ARE RUNNING DOWN HIS
FACE. NOT ICE-CREAM.

HE OPENS HIS EYES. HE HOLDS HIS ICE-CREAM OUT
TO ME.

**MAN**   You have please.

I DON'T REALLY FEEL LIKE ANOTHER ONE BUT I
TAKE IT AND EAT IT BECAUSE SOMEBODY HAS TO
DISPOSE OF IT.

THE MAN CLOSES HIS EYES AGAIN AND HUGS HIS
BRIEFCASE TO HIS CHEST. I TRY TO THINK WHAT I
CAN GIVE HIM IN RETURN FOR THREE ICE-CREAMS.

**ME**   I spy with my little eye something beginning
          with B.

THE MAN OPENS HIS EYES. HE LOOKS AT ME AND
THINKS FOR A BIT.

**MAN**  Bomb.

SOME OF THE OTHER PASSENGERS LOOK ALARMED
AGAIN. THE MAN POINTS OUT THE TRAIN WINDOW.
WE'RE STOPPED AT A STATION. I SEE WHAT HE'S
POINTING AT.

**ME**  You mean that old car parked over there with
rusty doors?

**MAN**  Yes.

**ME**  No.

THE MAN THINKS AGAIN.

**MAN**  Briefcase.

**ME**  Yes.

ME AND THE MAN PLAY I-SPY TILL HE GETS OFF
AT PENRITH. HE'S VERY GOOD AT IT, BUT ONLY
WITH WORDS STARTING WITH A, B AND C. ME
AND MUM WAVE TO HIM ON THE PLATFORM.
THEN TO MY SURPRISE MUM STARTS PLAYING
I-SPY WITH ME.

**MUM**  I spy with my little eye something beginning
with LM.

I LOOK AROUND THE CARRIAGE. I POINT TO A BLOKE
UP THE OTHER END WHO'S YELLING INTO HIS
PHONE.

**ME**     Loud mobile?

MUM POINTS TO HERSELF.

**MUM**    Lucky mum.

SHE GIVES ME A HUG. WE PLAY I-SPY FOR THE REST
OF THE TRIP. I'M GLAD I FORGOT MY MP3.

**THE END**

# Germ Meets Worm

'You need a holiday,' said Aristotle.

'No I don't,' said Blob.

Blob was sweeping so fast, Aristotle felt dizzy just watching his brother's broom.

'Yes you do,' said Aristotle. 'I can spot the signs.'

Blob was the tiredest-looking germ in the whole nostril. His body was flat and fatigue-wrinkled. His ectoplasm was grey. OK, some of the grey was dirt, but most of it was exhaustion.

'I haven't got time for a holiday,' grumbled Blob. He pointed to the vast space around them. 'I've got to sweep out this nostril, wash the nose hairs, clean out the mucus ducts, the smell equipment needs servicing, and if you don't pull your tendril out and get on with that dusting, I'll have to do that too.'

Aristotle sighed.

Or he would have done if nose germs could blow out air in an exasperated way. As they can't, he just

153

stuck out his bottom in an exasperated way.

'Give yourself a break, Blob,' said Aristotle. 'You don't have to do all the housework yourself.'

He pointed to the thousands of other nose germs in the nostril who were busily sweeping and dusting and washing and cleaning and whistling happily.

'Pah,' said Blob. 'They don't do it properly. There's only one germ around here who knows how to keep a human nostril clean and tidy, and that's mmpff . . .'

Blob wasn't able to finish because of the feather duster Aristotle stuffed into his speech duct.

'Listen to me,' said Aristotle. 'We've been slaving in this nostril most of our working lives. Four and a half hours at least. And we've never taken holidays. That means we're owed nearly twenty minutes off.'

Aristotle took the broom away from Blob, who didn't protest because he was busy pulling the feather duster out of his speech duct. And busy realising it was actually made from dust-mite armpit hair. And busy feeling sick.

'So,' said Aristotle, leaning Blob's broom against a pimple. 'Where shall we go for our holiday?'

Down in the stomach, Wilton the tummy worm was having a holiday he didn't need, or want, or like.

It was called his life.

'Please,' he begged the bacteria and enzymes and other stomach microbes hard at work all around him. 'I want to work too. I want to do something useful. I want a job.'

'Give it a rest, you jiffing harpic,' said a microbe foreman up to his waist in melting ice-cream. 'We've been through this a million times. You're a worm. We don't employ worms.' He yelled across the stomach cavity. 'Hey, can we get some digestive juices over here?'

'I'll get them,' said Wilton. 'Let me get them.'

'Stay where you are,' said the foreman. 'The squirties'll do it. It's their job.'

'But I want to help,' said Wilton.

'Surf and ajax,' said the foreman. 'Get it through your thick ectoplasm, you great fat lump. You're a worm. You don't have to work. You're a parasite. Enjoy it.'

Wilton curled up miserably.

He couldn't enjoy feeling bored and useless. All around him the vast tummy was gurgling with happy industry. Millions of lucky microbes leading enjoyable and satisfying lives doing interesting and important work.

Sorting the veggies from the meat.

Making neat piles of fingernail fragments.

Rounding up globules of fat and sending them off to the bloodstream where they belonged.

Wilton felt a familiar tickle in his mid-section.

'Half your luck,' said a cheery voice. 'Wish I had a life of leisure. I'd swap places with you any day.'

Wilton tried to stay calm. He reminded himself

he was very lucky to have a best friend living inside him, even if that best friend was sometimes a bit insensitive about jobs and tickling.

Algy's tiny microbe head appeared from inside one of Wilton's waste ducts.

'It's non-stop housework in here,' said Algy happily. 'Tidying your inside bits, cleaning your walls and floors, keeping all your vital organs neat. Then I turn my back and you've messed them all up again.'

Wilton looked enviously at his tiny friend.

'You're right,' he said. 'And I'm very grateful. But you don't have to do all the housework yourself. I could do some.'

'Don't be a dope,' said Algy gently. 'How are you going to sweep out your own insides? You haven't got any tendrils. How are you going to hold the broom?'

Wilton knew Algy was right.

'That's the real reason those tummy workers won't employ me,' said Wilton. 'If I had tendrils, I bet they'd give me a job.'

Algy shook his head.

'They won't employ you,' he said, 'because you're about a hundred times bigger than them and you won't fit in the tea room.'

Wilton sighed.

Or he would have done if tummy worms could exhale oxygen-related gases in a sad way. As they can't, he just let his bottom sag.

'Come on,' said Algy. 'Don't start feeling sorry for yourself. There must be a job somewhere for an oversized worm. We've just got to find it.'

Up in the nostril, the travel agent went amazed-shaped.

'A twenty-minute holiday?' he said to Aristotle and Blob. 'You are two lucky nose germs. The longest I've ever been away for is three minutes. And two minutes of that was the flights.'

'We've never had a holiday before,' said Aristotle. 'We'd like to go somewhere exotic and restful.'

'I've got just the thing,' said the travel agent. 'How about twenty luxurious minutes lazing by a pool?'

'Sounds good,' said Aristotle. 'Where are we travelling to?'

'Just over there,' said the travel agent, pointing. 'That pool of snot.'

Aristotle saw how many other holidaying germs were already splashing around in it.

He also saw what Blob was doing. Pulling cleaning gear out of his travel bag.

'Disgraceful,' said Blob. 'Look how cloudy that shallow end is. Filter must be clogged. I'll need to get at that with my scrubbing brush.'

'Have you got anywhere else?' said Aristotle hastily to the travel agent. 'Somewhere a bit more exotic and far away?'

'I certainly have,' said the travel agent. 'How

does a luxury golfing holiday sound? Eighteen hole course, all natural skin-pores, and it's way over the other side of the nostril.'

'Pah,' grumbled Blob. 'I've heard about the disgraceful state of the other side of the nostril. If we're going over there I'll have to take my broom.'

'Even more exotic,' said Aristotle to the travel agent. 'And even further away.'

The travel agent had a think.

'Aromatherapy retreat?' he said. 'Nose-hair hang-gliding? Mucus safari?'

'Somewhere,' said Aristotle, 'not in the nostril.'

The travel agent went alarmed-shaped.

'Oi,' yelled the angry digestion foreman. 'Harpic. Put that jiffing gravy down right now.'

Wilton winced and the drop of gravy he'd been trying to balance on his tail rolled off with a plop.

All around the stomach, thousands of bacteria glared at Wilton with that expression tummy workers get when they think you're trying to steal their job.

Algy peered nervously over Wilton's shoulder.

'Accept it, Wriggles,' he said. 'There just isn't a place for you in the digestion industry. Come on, let's go for a paddle in the spleen.'

Wilton didn't want to. All he did these days was paddle in the spleen. He was sick of it.

'There must be something useful I can do,'

he said. 'I can't swim, so that rules out the blood industry. And I haven't got a sense of rhythm, so I'd be hopeless in the heart industry.'

Algy hated seeing his friend so unhappy.

'You're big and strong,' he said to Wilton. 'Maybe in the spleen they'll let you put out the deckchairs and beach umbrellas.'

Wilton wasn't listening.

He had just noticed something very unusual. Two strange microbes were speeding down the stomach wall in a rental saliva bubble.

Wilton stiffened in alarm.

'Nose germs,' he said. 'Look, you can tell, they've got noses. And one of them's armed.'

'It's not a weapon,' said Algy quietly. 'It's a broom.'

'The other one's got a camera,' said Wilton.

'Tourists,' said Algy.

'They could be the advance party for an invasion force,' said Wilton. 'That's what happened when the bottom germs invaded.'

Wilton looked anxiously around the stomach. The tummy workers were all working busily. Some of them were giving the nose germs a glance, but that was all.

'They're leaving it to me to stop the invaders,' said Wilton.

'Are you sure?' said Algy.

'You said it yourself,' replied Wilton. 'I'm big and strong. I was made for this sort of work. Fighting to the death with violent invaders.'

'I didn't say that last bit,' squeaked Algy, hastily retreating into one of Wilton's waste ducts.

'Hold tight,' said Wilton.

'Try not to be too violent,' pleaded Algy. 'I've just tidied all your internal organs.'

'I'll be as violent as I have to,' said Wilton, wriggling towards the nose germs. 'To get the job done.'

Aristotle parked the saliva bubble and peered nervously through the windscreen.

He was beginning to see why the travel agent hadn't wanted to book this trip for them. Why they'd had to tickle him until he'd given in.

The tummy was huge and crowded and noisy and dirty and not in the slightest bit exotic.

'I think we might have made a mistake,' said Aristotle to Blob.

'No we haven't,' said Blob. 'This is definitely the tummy. See, there's the back of the belly button.'

'I mean it doesn't seem like a very good place for a relaxing holiday,' said Aristotle. 'Look at the rough way those tummy germs are flinging that food around.'

'Disgraceful,' said Blob. 'This place needs a complete sweep out from top to bottom.'

He grabbed his broom and started to get out of the bubble.

'Wait,' said Aristotle, grabbing him. 'Stay here. I don't like the look of the locals.'

'They're only tummy germs,' said Blob. 'They're just microbes like us, only messier.'

'I don't mean the tummy germs,' said Aristotle.

With a trembling tendril he pointed at the huge worm wriggling towards them and looming over them in a very determined and possibly violent way.

'Arghhh,' squeaked Blob. 'This wasn't in the brochure.'

Then everything went brown.

It was the biggest lump of chocolate Wilton and Algy had ever seen.

'Wow,' said Algy, peeping out from inside Wilton. 'A lump of chocolate bigger than a worm. Now I've seen everything.'

Wilton tried to stay calm.

The giant brown lump had dropped from the throat tube at the top of the tummy and landed on the saliva bubble with a splat, completely burying the two nose germs.

'That,' said Algy, 'was a really silly place to park.'

Wilton tried to see if the nose germs were all right. Suddenly he was feeling a bit confused about his new job. It seemed a bit unfair to be fighting two nose germs to the death when they were buried in chocolate.

'Come on,' he said to Algy. 'We'd better get them out.'

Wilton started burrowing into the mound of

soggy chocolate, his whole body rippling with the effort.

Algy helped.

'Faster,' said Wilton. 'They're buried alive.'

'I'm only a small microbe,' said Algy. 'I'm eating as fast as I can.'

'Oi,' yelled an angry voice. 'You two jiffing drainos leave that chocolate alone. Pine-o-clean, how many times do I have to tell you?'

Wilton pulled his head out of the chocolate and glared down at the foreman.

'This isn't work,' he said. 'It's a rescue.'

The foreman didn't looked convinced. Wilton drew himself up to his full length. The foreman, noting that Wilton was about a hundred times bigger than him, backed off.

'I'm watching you, ajax,' he muttered to Wilton. 'I don't mind you mucking around with tourists, but if I catch you doing any food processing, I'll be down on you like a tonne of marshmallows.'

That's when Algy had the idea.

He stopped eating the chocolate and stared at Wilton. He even forgot there was more chocolate to eat – that's how amazing the idea was.

'I can't get over how clean and tidy this place is,' said Blob, gazing around inside Wilton. 'I couldn't make this place cleaner and tidier if I tried. Though I probably will try a bit later.'

He took another sip of his chocolate cocktail

and relaxed in his deckchair.

Algy glowed with pride.

Aristotle glowed too, with relief. He settled back on a wonderfully comfortable sofa made from the softest skin cells he'd ever sat on.

At last, he and Blob were having a real break.

What a nice tummy worm and tummy microbe, thought Aristotle. More like holiday resort hosts than vicious killers.

'This is such a great spot for a holiday,' he said gratefully to Algy. 'It's so quiet and peaceful in here. And you've done wonders with the décor.'

Algy glowed even more.

'I couldn't go wrong,' he said modestly. 'Wilton's so roomy and his internal organs were made for the place.'

Wilton listened contentedly to the chatter inside him.

What nice nose germs, he thought. More like polite houseguests than violent invaders.

'Everyone OK in there?' he called. 'Algy, let them play table tennis if they want to. I don't mind, I like the tickly feeling.'

It was the happiest twenty minutes of Aristotle and Blob's whole lives, and they felt like it would never end.

But like all gloriously long holidays, it finally did.

While Algy went off to organise a rental stomach-gas bubble for their return journey to the nose, Aristotle and Blob climbed up onto Wilton's shoulder to thank him. And to let him know they hadn't had anything from the mini-bar.

'We had a wonderful stay,' said Aristotle.

'You are the best holiday destination in the whole world,' said Blob. 'And when we tell our travel agent about you and your very reasonable rates, you're going to be the most booked out.'

Wilton grinned.

Or he would have done if worms had grin muscles. As they don't, he let gentle ripples of contentment run along his whole body so each waste duct was briefly stretched into a little smile.

If all the future guests were as nice as these two nose germs, Wilton couldn't wait.

'You won't mind?' said Aristotle. 'Being booked out all the time?'

'Of course not,' said Wilton happily. 'It's my job.'

# Snugglepots And Cuddlepies

Those Cuddlepies are scum.

I'm sorry, I know it's not a nice thing to say. Mum would probably punish me if she heard me. Stop me watching *Australian Idol* for a week or something. Mum believes we should behave with compassion and respect towards other human beings, including Cuddlepies.

But I can't help it.

They are scum.

Wait till I tell you what a bunch of them did today.

I don't know what they were taught at those Cuddlepie Early Learning Centres, but it sure wasn't compassion or respect. Or nice smiles. We did nice smiles in the first week at my Snugglepot Kindy Solutions Centre. It wasn't easy because I was only one and a half, but I did the homework and I passed nice smiles in first term.

OK, I know that's boasting, but I'm proud to be a Snugglepot even after all these years, and Mum reckons it's OK to be proud of yourself if you deserve it.

'Give yourself a pat on the back, Paloma,' Mum said to me a few days ago when I told her I'd been chosen for the year six netball team. She asked me to do the patting myself cause she was delayed in Perth at a meeting and probably wouldn't be home till after midnight.

After we hung up I gave myself a pat.

I could have asked Dad to do it, but he was rushing around getting ready to go to his men's group. He was in a flap because he had to give them a talk on his experiences as a workaholic, so I didn't want to distract him.

I didn't mind. Patting myself on the back is another thing I learned at kindy. They teach it at all the Snugglepot Kindy Solutions Centres around the country, so if you ever see somebody patting themselves on the back, they're probably a Snugglepot.

That bunch of Cuddlepies who attacked me and Cheri today weren't patting themselves on the back.

Or smiling nicely.

I was on my way to school with Cheri and we ducked into Northpoint to check out the lipsticks in Pricerite. Mum reckons I'm too young to wear lipstick, but she's a big supporter of people planning ahead in their lives.

Cheri was sniffing a Dusky Peach tester when I gave her a nudge.

'Cuddlepies,' I whispered.

There were about six of them coming out of Subway. You can spot Cuddlepies a mile off when you know the signs and you've had them in your class since year one.

Tyson Phelps was at the front. He saw us and pointed.

'Check the Snugglepots buying the ugly sticks,' he jeered.

The others all laughed and did that cruel Cuddlepie sneer. Including Gale Bishop who always rubs her tomato sauce on her lips to look sexy when she thinks nobody's looking.

Cheri pretended to ignore them, which was sensible. Cuddlepies can be vicious if you get them worked up.

I wasn't sensible.

'She's not buying, cretin brains, she's just looking,' I said to the Cuddlepies. 'And anyway, she's not a Snugglepot, so rack off.'

Tyson Phelps did another Cuddlepie sneer.

'Don't lie,' he said. 'Why would she hang around a smelly Snugglepot like you if she wasn't one herself?'

Cheri put the lipstick down and turned and faced the Cuddlepies and put her hands on her hips. She's pretty short, but she read somewhere that putting your hands on your hips makes you look bigger and tougher.

'I hang around her because she's my friend,' said Cheri. 'You heard her, rack off.'

When Cheri's defending you, her face goes really pink and she gets asthma and can't breathe properly. But it doesn't stop her. And do you know what's even more amazing? She's not even a Snugglepot. Her parents didn't send her to a Snugglepot Kindy Solutions Centre. They didn't send her anywhere. When she started in year one, she confessed to me that she'd never been to a single Kindy Centre or Long Daycare Playschool or Early Years Speed-growth Camp or anything.

Poor kid.

'Rack off yourself,' replied Tyson Phelps to Cheri.

You can see the sort of wit they teach at those Cuddlepie so-called Early Learning Centres.

I turned my back on the whole lot of them because by this stage Cheri was bending over and wheezing and I had to help her find her puffer in her school bag.

While we searched, I felt cold sloppy things hitting my face.

Tyson and the others were flicking bits of Subway at us. Turkey loaf and salad extender and slices of pickle that really sting if they hit you in the eye.

I haven't been able to get much work done this morning here in class. I've just been sitting here thinking about them doing that.

Only Cuddlepies would attack a sick kid like

Cheri and do it with really vinegary sandwich fillings.

See what I mean about scum?

At 4pm I had my first netball match ever against another school.

It was a very big occasion for me.

And, as it turned out, a very confusing one.

The hall was full of parents. Mum couldn't be there, she's in Cairns at a meeting, and Dad had an appointment at his therapist, but I didn't mind because I had Cheri. She's not allowed to play netball on account of her wheezing, but she's a fantastic supporter as long as she doesn't get too carried away and pass out.

I was on the bench for the first quarter. New team members always are.

Cheri came and sat next to me and we tried to work out which people on the visiting team were Cuddlepies.

I hadn't met any of them before. Their school is about ten suburbs away. But you can spot a Cuddlepie on the netball court a mile off if you know the signs.

Rough play is one.

And sneering at the umpire behind her back.

With this visiting team it was really hard to tell. They played tough but fair. When the umpire blew her whistle against them, they copped it. Some even with nice smiles.

'Amazing,' I whispered to Cheri. 'They must all be Snugglepots.'

Cheri didn't say anything. She'd spent most of the match so far crouched down rummaging in her bag. Probably looking for her spare puffer, I thought, in case the last quarter was a nail biter.

I studied the visiting players more closely.

There was one, their wing defence, skinny with long bleached dreads, who kept glancing over at me and Cheri.

That made me suspicious. Cuddlepies reckon they can spot Snugglepots a mile off too.

'I reckon she's a Cuddlepie,' I muttered to Cheri. 'Plotting some way to get me next quarter when I'm playing.'

Cheri still didn't say anything.

Just looked worried.

So I figured I must be right.

Then the first quarter ended and an amazing thing happened. The Cuddlepie wing defence girl trotted over to us, bold as really bold lipstick.

'G'day Cheri,' she said. 'I thought it was you.'

Cheri gave her the sort of pasty smile she gives adults when she's trying to persuade them she feels better than she really does.

The girl saw me staring and gave me a friendly grin.

'Me and Cheri used to know each other,' she said. 'We went to the same Cuddlepie Early Learning Centre.'

I felt like a netball had just whacked me in the head.

Cheri?

A Cuddlepie?

Cheri was looking like she was having a major attack, eyes wide and mouth open, except she wasn't wheezing.

I grabbed at a wild thought. Perhaps this was all lies. An evil Cuddlepie plot by this other girl to break me and Cheri up. But if it was a lie, why wasn't Cheri denying it?

The girl stared at me with a friendly frown.

'You weren't at our Centre, were you?' she asked.

I shook my head.

'Didn't think so,' she said. 'Which Cuddlepie Centre did you go to?'

Cheri was looking panicked now and that's when I knew the only Cuddlepie lie here today is the one Cheri has been telling me for the last five-and-a-half years.

I glared at them both.

'I went to a Snugglepot Kindy Solutions Centre,' I said.

The girl took a step back. She stared at me like I was a lump of dog poo in a netball uniform.

'Gross,' she said to Cheri. 'Why are you hanging around with a slimy Snugglepot?'

Cheri looked at us both helplessly. I'd never seen her lost for words before, except when she was slipping into unconsciousness.

171

The girl turned and walked away.

Cheri grabbed me and tried to say something.

I didn't want to hear it.

The umpire blew her whistle for the second quarter and Mrs West our coach came over and told me I was playing goal shooter.

The rest of the match was a blur. I scored some goals and the Cuddlepie wing defence girl fouled me every chance she got and at half time I stayed in the team huddle and we won I think.

I tried to concentrate on the match but my dazed mind just kept thinking the same thought.

My best friend is a Cuddlepot.

I mean Cuddlepie.

See how confused I am?

At the end of the match as I hurried towards the changing room, Cheri came up to me. She looked like she'd been crying.

'I'm sorry,' she mumbled miserably. 'I hated lying to you but I just wanted to be your friend.'

I pushed past her into the changing room and locked myself in a cubicle and I've been here ever since.

Confused.

I should be furious with Cheri for pulling a typical low Cuddlepie stunt and lying to me. That is so typical of them.

But I'm sitting here trying to be angry with her, and I just can't do it.

When I saw how upset she was I wanted to

put my arms round her. That's partly because I'm a Snugglepot and I have compassion and respect towards other human beings, but mostly because she's my best friend.

This is weird.

I'm feeling all warm and loving towards a Cuddlepie.

OK, here's what I reckon has happened. Cheri has spent so much time with me over the past five-and-a-half years that she's turned into a Snugglepot.

Yes, of course, that must be it.

Phew, I'm feeling better already.

Here's what I'm going to do. Go out there right now and give Cheri a hug and say sorry for ignoring her. It might be a bit hard for her at first, discovering she's a Snugglepot, but she's a pretty amazing person so I reckon she'll cope.

Here I go.

Hang on.

Oh, no.

What if it happened the other way round?

Over the past five-and-a-half years I've spent just as much time with Cheri as she has with me.

What if I've turned into a . . .?

No way. I can't believe I'm even thinking this. It couldn't happen. It's impossible. Me turn into a Cuddlepie? Not a chance.

Except if I'm a Snugglepot and Cheri's a Cuddlepie, why do we care about each other so much?

Of course.

Yes.

I know what's happened.

Why didn't I realise it before?

OK, here I go. I'm on my way to give Cheri a hug and explain the whole thing to her.

I know.

People will laugh.

Specially that Cuddlepie lot. The Snugglepots probably will too.

But me and Cheri won't care because we'll have our friendship. We'll stand side by side and proudly tell the world the truth.

We're not Snugglepots.

Or Cuddlepies.

We're a mixture.

We're Snugglepies.

Or, if Cheri prefers, Cuddlepots.

And anyone who says we're not, they're scum.

# Why My Dad Could Be Prime Minister

My dad could be Prime Minister because he's kind to animals and he knows good jokes and he loves Australian food including noodles and he lets the neighbours borrow our lawnmower and he doesn't snore and he can wiggle his ears and he's modest after he's put a fire out in somebody's house and he gives other people his seat on the bus except if they're hooligans and he only cries if a movie is really sad or it's got onions in it and he does his own ironing and he trims his own nose hairs and he can bend metal with his bare hands and he's got heaps of friends and he can lift a telly if it needs rescuing and he knows quite a lot of cartoon voices and he's good at putting band-aids on cut fingers and he gives you a hug after.

But he does have three bad habits he would have to change if he was going to be Prime Minister.

One is, he sometimes gets words wrong.

Like tonight.

Dad was reading the politics part of the paper, which he does a lot, and suddenly he looks at the clock and sees we're still up.

'OK, you kids,' he says. 'Let's have a new law in this house. Let's call it the Bedtime Choices Act.'

Me and Beth and Charlie all cheer. We like the idea of choosing our own bedtime. It means we can finish the Sim city we're working on. But most of all we want to wait up till Mum gets home.

'Agreed?' says Dad.

'Yes,' yell me and Beth and Charlie.

'OK,' says Dad. 'I want you all in bed in three minutes. Which is just enough time to save your game, do your teeth and give me a very big kiss.'

I look at Dad, confused.

He does breathe in a bit of smoke at work sometimes from the burning buildings. Maybe it's affected his brain.

'But,' I stammer. 'You said . . .'

'Bedtime Choices,' grins Dad. 'Your bedtime, my choice.'

Me and Beth and Charlie stare at him.

'Not fair,' wail Beth and Charlie.

I wonder if I should explain to Dad that he's got it wrong. I decide not to. It might take more than three minutes.

'We want to stay up till Mum gets home,' I say quietly.

Dad's face goes serious.

'I know you do, Jack,' he says. 'But she might be home pretty late. Very late, actually. As you know, she's gone to the movies. I'm not sure what time her movie ends.'

A small flicker of worry starts in the bottom of my guts. Like one of those little flames that can grow into a huge fire.

Why doesn't Dad know what time Mum's movie ends? The movie times are on the internet. I bet the Prime Minister always knows what time his wife's movie ends.

Maybe Mum hasn't gone where she told us she was going. To the local movie theatre. Maybe she's gone to that big multiplex, the one on the very busy dangerous road. Maybe I was right when she was saying goodbye earlier and I saw that strange look on her face.

The guilty one.

I wondered then if something was going on and I'm wondering it again now.

'Two and a half minutes,' says Dad.

As I lead Beth and Charlie off to the bathroom I wonder if Dad has got the words 'gone to the movies' wrong just like he got the words 'bedtime choices' wrong.

If he has, that means Mum could be anywhere.

I don't ask Dad about it in case it upsets Beth and Charlie.

That's the thing about having a dad who's a firefighter. Who risks his life every day at work.

Who you can never be totally sure will come home safely.

You grow up to be a kid who worries a lot.

I can't sleep.

The worry flame is getting bigger and my insides are burning.

I get out of bed and creep into the living room. Dad is asleep on the sofa in front of the telly. The clock says 11.47.

Mum still isn't home.

'Dad,' I say, giving him a prod.

He opens his eyes.

'Is Mum in hospital having a serious operation?' I ask.

Dad stares at me. Then he pulls me onto his lap.

'No, mate,' he says. 'She's not.'

I can see he's telling the truth. He's got little crinkles round his eyes. Mum calls them crows feet. Dad calls them heat lines. I call them truth crinkles.

'Is she having a love affair with another bloke?' I ask.

Dad doesn't grin.

Even though it's a very crazy idea, he knows how awful it would be if she was.

'No, Jack,' he says. 'Definitely not.'

He's still telling the truth.

I tell him my last worry. That's the great thing about a dad like him, you can. If I was voting for a

Prime Minister, I'd always vote for one who lets you sit on their lap and tell them your worries.

'Has Mum committed some crime,' I say, 'and she's gone to hand herself in?'

Now Dad does smile. But he's shaking his head and his truth crinkles are still there.

'So Mum really has just gone to the movies?' I say.

Perhaps tonight our local cinema is showing all six *Star Wars* movies back to back.

'She really has,' says Dad.

I stare at him.

Something has happened to his eyes. The truth crinkles have vanished. He's not telling the truth.

This is the second bad habit he'll have to change. He doesn't tell lies much, but you can't tell them at all if you want to be Prime Minister.

I don't have that thought at the time.

I'm too panicked.

Plus, one second after I discover from Dad's face that Mum isn't at the movies, she walks in. Very slowly. Like she's in pain. She looks even more pained when she sees I'm up.

I stare at her, a worry bushfire ripping through me.

Mum's shirt is unbuttoned and underneath it I can see a big bandage round her chest.

The other bad habit Dad will have to change if he's ever Prime Minister is the one where he says he's thinking about other people when he's really thinking about himself.

That's what happened tonight when Mum walked in all bandaged up.

I gasped at the sight of her.

'Love,' says Dad to Mum. 'Are you OK? You look terrible. Tell Jack you're OK.'

What he really means is 'tell me you're OK'.

Dad looks like his insides are ablaze with worry too.

'Relax, both of you,' says Mum. 'I'm fine.'

She doesn't look fine.

'What is it?' I say. 'What happened?'

I try to prepare myself for really bad news. Like she's been shot. Or stabbed. Or had her appendix out.

Mum hesitates. I can see she wishes I was asleep. But I'm not.

'It's just a tattoo,' she says.

My brain must be a bit heat-affected from the burning worry because I don't get it at first.

'A tattoo?' I say.

'That's all,' she says.

Then I do get it. Dad's had a tattoo for years and Mum's always saying how she'd like one.

I wasn't born when Dad got his tattoo, but he's told me how it hurt a lot and went scabby for the first few days.

'Show me,' I say to Mum.

She and Dad look at each other. They know it's

the only way to get me back to bed without a fuss, so Mum shows me.

'Yuk,' I say as Dad unwinds the bandage. Mum's back is red and swollen and definitely starting to go scabby.

Then I see what the tattoo is.

It's me and Beth and Charlie and Mum and Dad. We're all smiling out of the middle of Mum's back with our arms round each other. I think the tattoo artist must have used the photo from when Dad volunteered to fight the bushfires in Gippsland and we all went with him to keep him company in the motel.

'That's great,' I say.

It is.

Tattoos are permanent.

Like families.

Mum's tattoo isn't as action-packed as Dad's, but not many tattoos are. He's got flames shooting up out of the back of his undies and a big squirting hose coiled round his shoulders.

People would be so impressed to have a Prime Minister with a tattoo like that.

Mum works in a deli, which I think is why she didn't make her tattoo about her job. When people saw the ham and salami, they might think the tattoo hadn't healed.

'Why did you say you were going to the movies?' I ask Mum.

She looks a bit embarrassed.

'I was worried I might chicken out,' she says. 'You know, when I got to the tattoo parlour and saw the needles. That's why I asked Dad not to tell you where I was going. If I didn't get it done, I didn't want you kids to think I was a coward.'

'We'd never think that,' I say to her.

It's true, we wouldn't. In the motel in Gippsland Mum pulled a huge splinter out of Dad's armpit with her teeth.

'I knew you wouldn't chicken out,' says Dad, giving her a kiss.

That's another reason why Dad could be Prime Minister. He has total faith in people. You have to when you're sharing a hose and a ladder. Plus he's incredibly gentle at putting a bandage back onto a new tattoo. As he does it, Mum doesn't even wince.

And he's generous.

'I like yours even more than mine,' he says to Mum.

His truth crinkles are there the whole time.

I'm not sure if Dad would ever want to be Prime Minister on account of he loves being a firefighter heaps, but if he does give it a crack one day he'll be really well qualified if he can kick those few little bad habits.

I used to want Dad to be Prime Minister so we wouldn't have to worry about him so much. It's a known fact that very few Prime Ministers have ever perished in fires in other people's houses.

But I don't think I'll be worrying about Dad

quite so much now. If I feel those tummy flames coming on, I'll just ask Mum to take her shirt off so I can have a squiz at her back.

Oh, there is one more thing Dad knows how to do that I reckon would make him a brilliant Prime Minister.

He did it just now.

I'm back in bed and almost off to sleep, and Dad pokes his head round my bedroom door.

'That bull I told you about Mum being at the movies,' he whispers.

'Don't worry about it, Dad,' I murmur.

'No,' he says, 'I want to apologise.'

He doesn't have to because I understand, but he does anyway.

'Sorry,' he says.

I reckon I'd vote for him even if he wasn't my dad.

# So Unjust

Samantha loved reading stories.

The part of each story she liked best was the twist at the end. That funny and unexpected moment when everything is suddenly OK and the main character ends up delighted and relieved and a bit stunned all at the same time.

'Yes,' chuckled Samantha as she read how the puzzled owner of the giggling limping parrot discovered that the parrot's previous owner had been very ticklish, specially near his wooden leg.

'Good one,' laughed Samantha when the forgetful boy who swallowed his iPod found his memory was improving.

'Brilliant,' she chortled when the airport terminal that had always been jealous of the planes got blown up and discovered it could fly too.

Samantha loved those twists.

But each time she read one, sprawled on her

bedroom floor, a tiny part of her always ended up feeling sad.

The truth was, much as she loved her shelf of neatly arranged books packed with twist-enriched stories, they weren't quite enough.

What Samantha wanted more than anything was a twist or two in her own life.

Nothing huge like discovering Mum and Dad, who both loved Mars Bars, were Martians. Or having her teacher Ms Quigly, who could whistle through her teeth, fall in love with her dentist and not be able to stop whistling the ring tone of the dentist's dead wife's mobile. Or saying 'to die for' a lot and then actually dying.

Nothing that big. Just a few small fun twists that would make life more interesting.

But they never happened.

Samantha's life was twistless.

Then one Saturday morning she read a story and understood why.

It wasn't the best story she'd ever read, and the twist was a bit ordinary. It was about a boy who swallowed a tea bag and then had to do a parachute jump. The boy was terrified he'd land in a tree and hang there jiggling and never be rescued. So he swallowed some coffee beans, ones that had been ground because that's where he wanted to land. But when he jumped out of the plane his parachute didn't open, so he quickly swallowed another tea bag and his fall was broken by the shade cloth over the staff BBQ area of a teapot factory.

Wow, thought Samantha. So that's how it works. You have to make twists happen.

For the rest of that day, Samantha worked hard to make twists happen in her own life.

Instead of trying to have a conversation with Dad, which she did every Saturday morning, and instead of getting frustrated while Dad read his paper and only replied in grunts, which he did every Saturday morning, Samantha went down to the shopping centre and juggled half-litre milk cartons outside Officeworks.

She hoped that a newspaper photographer would notice her. And that her photo would be in the paper the following Saturday morning. And that Dad would see it just as he was in the middle of not paying her very much attention.

That, she was pretty sure, would be a twist.

But unfortunately the photographer from the local paper was doing his first parachute jump that day and wasn't around.

Passers-by were impressed, though. They'd never seen a girl juggling half-litre milk cartons before. They thought Samantha was busking, and dropped money at her feet, over $150 in total. But Samantha knew that didn't count as a twist because she'd put the plastic bucket there herself.

After lunch, while Mum was sewing, which she did every Saturday afternoon, Samantha asked if Mum would teach her to sew, which she did every Saturday afternoon, and Mum, as usual, said not until Samantha was older because the sewing machine was a very expensive one, and dangerous.

So Samantha went back down to the shops and spent her busking money on a chainsaw.

She hid it under her bed and spent a happy few hours looking forward to next Saturday. At which time, when Mum said that the sewing machine was dangerous, Samantha planned to show her the chainsaw and say, 'No, Mum, this is dangerous.'

It would be a satisfying moment, but it still wouldn't be a twist because Dad's birthday was the week after and he'd been saying he wanted a chainsaw for ages.

Samantha sighed. It was Saturday evening now and she still hadn't made a twist happen.

Mum and Dad were watching TV, which they did every Saturday night, and only replying with vague murmurs when she spoke to them.

Samantha thought about going next door and strangling the elderly couple who lived there, Mr and Mrs Kemp.

That would be a twist, because Mum and Dad were watching Midsomer Murders.

But she didn't. Strangling elderly neighbours wasn't a good thing to do, even though they were grouchy and threw pill bottles at her when she went into their garden to get her ball.

Samantha decided to call it a day.

'Night, Mum,' she said. 'Night, Dad.'

They both murmured something vague.

Samantha got into bed and re-read the story about the boy and the tea bag. Had she missed something? Some important clue about how to make twists happen? She didn't think so.

As her eyelids got heavy, she had a hopeful thought. That even as she was closing the book, a local parachutist, making his or her first night jump, would lose control of the parachute and crash through the roof of the house and dent Mum's sewing machine and Mum would be sad she hadn't let Samantha have a go while it still worked.

But nothing like that happened.

Samantha slid the book under her pillow and her last thought before she drifted off was that perhaps she would never find a way to make a twist happen.

Unless, she thought dreamily, an author who's looking for a story idea with a twist at the end finds out about me. And is fascinated by a girl who loves twists in stories but never has them in her own life.

Now that would be a twist, thought Samantha, if I ended up in a story myself.

# A Word From Morris

G'day. I hope you enjoy these stories. I had fun writing lots of new characters. I also had a great time going on new adventures with some of my old friends.

In case you haven't met those old friends before, here's where they first appeared in my previous books.

Ro and her dad from '101 Text Messages You Must Read Before You Die' can be found looking out for each other and sometimes exasperating each other in *Blabber Mouth*, *Sticky Beak* and *Gift Of The Gab*.

In *Second Childhood*, Mark from 'Ashes To Ashes' gets into even more strife than he does in this book.

If you think Jake's mission is impossible in 'Mission Impossible', wait till you see what he's faced with in *Adults Only*.

Ginger from 'Good Dog' has some other interesting animal friends in *Teacher's Pet*. So does Ned from 'My First Ever Go At Bomb Disposal'.

'Give Peas A Chance' isn't Ben's only attempt to

save the world. He's at it again in *The Other Facts Of Life*.

In *Misery Guts*, *Worry Warts* and *Puppy Fat*, Tracy from 'Think Big' is just as outspoken and gutsy, even though her friend Keith sometimes wishes she wasn't.

Kevin from 'Paparazzi' fails to be cool once again in *Doubting Thomas*.

If you'd like to spend more time in the microbiological world of 'Germ Meets Worm', you can join Wilton and Algy on an epic journey in *Worm Story*, and share a very surprising visit next door with Aristotle and Blob in *Aristotle's Nostril*.

And finally, although Dougie's dad doesn't appear much in 'Greenhouse Gas', you can get to know him as a kid in *Belly Flop*, and see that Dougie and Grandpa aren't the only ones in that family who'll try to change the weather to solve a problem.

Happy reading, and thanks for sharing my stories,

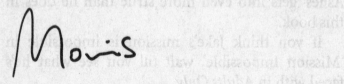

# Join Limpy the cane toad in three hilarious, heroic adventures

TOAD RAGE TOAD HEAVEN TOAD AWAY

Illustrations © Mike Millman

From the Sydney Olympics to the Amazon jungle, Limpy just can't help getting into some sticky situations.

Be warned – it could get messy!

'A hilarious high-speed read . . . a real ripper!'
– *Sunday Times*

puffin.co.uk

morrisgleitzman.com

# Two Weeks with the Queen

Colin Mudford is on a quest. His brother, Luke, has cancer and the doctors in Australia don't seem to be able to cure him. Colin reckons it's up to him to find the best doctor in the world.

**How better to do this than asking the Queen to help ...?**

# Teacher's Pet

'Ginger, Ginger, Ginger,' said Mr Napier. 'How did a nice family like yours end up with a person like you in it?'

Trouble seems to follow Ginger around, especially as her best friend is a fierce-looking stray dog.

'Morris Gleitzman has a rare gift for writing very funny stories'
– *Guardian*

'Readers can't get enough of him'
– *Independent*